HIS ...
AS EASILY AS A WORN PIECE OF TWINE.

With a low groan, Doug dug his hands into her soft curls, ground his mouth against hers.

She turned, arching toward him, into his arms, and tumbled off the sofa. Doug rolled with her, softening her fall with his body. Jan didn't seem to realize she now lay sprawled against him on the floor. Her hands were against his chest, her breath mingled with his.

Doug ran his hands down her spine, touched bare shoulder blades, slim waist, and moved lower over her hips. Jan squirmed with pleasure.

"Mmm," she purred again. "What took you so long?"

Doug's mouth moved down her throat in a sensuous glide. Hot and damp and oh, so good.

"Mechanicals," he murmured against her collarbone.

"You're very good at these mechanics," Jan said in a sigh.

"I'm feeling inspired, very inspired," Doug whispered.

BETH HENDERSON

Fortune And Folly

ZEBRA BOOKS
KENSINGTON PUBLISHING CORP.

ZEBRA BOOKS

are published by

Kensington Publishing Corp.
475 Park Avenue South
New York, NY 10016

Copyright © 1992 by Beth Henderson

First printing: November, 1992

Printed in the United States of America

*To Janet Hafner and Joan Horrigan
for lending me their profession,
and in honor of the
28th Anniversary of the
founding of the
Society for Prevention of Cruelty
to Lunchbags.*

Prologue

The old man watched the young girl as she leafed through the hefty book. She balanced it on her knees, her head bent forward as she peered at each page. Her dark curls tumbled around her rosy cheeks.

He smiled to himself. He hadn't seen much of Janelle in her short life. Mostly because his nephew had a backbone. Unlike the rest of the Ingrahams, Jan's father kept his distance and refused to grovel. It had only been through Beatrice's manipulations that Janelle was sitting across the table from him now. Simon knew what to expect of the girl's aunt. He wasn't so sure about his great-niece herself.

It was hard to believe his nephew's little girl was growing up. She was twelve years old but already the color in her cheeks was pure woman's fury.

Jan snapped the dictionary shut and put it aside next to the game board. "There's no such word," she claimed, her blue eyes fairly spitting at him.

Simon Ingraham settled himself in his chair and reached for his cheap-smelling cigar. "Didn't your father ever tell you to respect your elders, Jannie?

7

If I say there's such a word, you better believe there is."

Jan glared at him over the table. She pointed at the Scrabble board. "I looked it up, Uncle Simon. In *your* dictionary! W-Y-M isn't a word."

"Sure it is. And since both the W and M are on double-letter score squares, it's worth a whopping eighteen points. Put it down, girl," he insisted gesturing toward the tally sheet with his cigar.

Jan wrinkled her nose as a cloud of noxious smoke wafted her way. "You made it up," she snarled. "Just like you did those other three words."

"I'm just following your lead, honey," Simon said. "I didn't raise a fuss when you wanted to misspell that color word."

"Misspell!"

My, my, Simon mused. She sure was a fetching little thing when she got her dander up.

She fought to regain control. He liked that about her, too. Found he liked a good deal about this slip of a girl. Took after her dad. Not in looks so much, but in the way she didn't take his guff. Shame they were the only Ingrahams who stood up to him. The rest of the family had rubber backbones. He might like the rest of his clan a touch more if they showed steel in their makeup like this feisty great-niece.

Jan's hands were still clenched in fury but her voice was as cool as that of a duchess. "There is no law that says you can't use the alternate spelling of a word. G-R-E-Y is the British spelling."

8

Simon puffed on his cigar. That's what he liked about Scrabble. It tended to get people on their high horses. Or it did the way he played it. Unless, of course, they were relatives with an eye on his money.

"You gonna play or argue, girl?"

She fumed a bit more then chose two more anonymous letters from the kitty. "If WYM is a word, what's it mean?" Jan demanded.

Simon blew three perfect smoke rings and watched them float in the still afternoon air. "Means something that comes on you sudden, like a craving for ice cream."

Jan barely glanced up from contemplating her letters. "That's W-H-I-M."

"To you. Not to me," Simon said with aplomb. "Ought to get rid of all those letters that sound the same and just have a single one stand for a sound. No more wondering if a word had a C or a K, or used an F or a PH. Simple word like wife should be spelled Y-F."

"That's stupid," she declared, her eyes barely glancing up to meet his.

"Economic, I'd say," Simon insisted. "You got anything to add to this board? I'm getting impatient to dazzle you with my next word."

"Made up again, I'll bet," Jan mumbled under her breath.

"I heard that."

She glared at her rack of letters, then at the board. Simon could almost see her eyes raking over his earlier contributions. He tried like hell to stay away from using real words. They ruined his enjoyment of the game.

Simon leaned back in his chair, and stared at the bucolic landscape over the sofa. His mother had been partial to it. He'd always been partial to money. And more than set to hang on to every last nickel he'd made.

He turned his attention back to the girl. "Bea says you're already thinking about college," Simon said conversationally. "What're you planning on studying? Business like your old uncle?"

Jan gave him a steady gaze before answering. "Art."

"Art." He mused over the word a bit. "Art don't pay the bills, girl. In my experience, the artist has to be dead before anyone cares for the stuff. But then, I suppose that's why you're here? Beatrice probably told you if you played up to me, I'd cough up your tuition."

Her silence told Simon he'd guessed right.

He studied the tip of his cigar. "I just might if you majored in finance."

"Like you, huh."

He smiled at the animosity in her voice. "College is expensive, Jannie," he continued. "You think on it. After you finish pondering over that damn rack of letters."

"I don't need to think about it. You couldn't pay me enough to take finance courses," she declared. "I don't need your old money. I'll get a scholarship or a job at McDonald's. I'll get by on my own.

And—" She nearly crowed the word. "—I'm going to win this game."

In quick succession she arranged all of her remaining small wooden letters in a row to form the word: Q-A-J-E-Z.

Simon puffed up a cloud of smoke to hide the amusement in his eyes. "Qajez? What the hell kind of foreign word is that?"

It was Jan's turn to lean back in her chair, her long, jean-clad legs stretched out. She gave him a superior smile. "One that follows your wonderful example, Uncle Simon," she cooed. "It's a five-letter word that means I tromped you good," she said smugly. "Thirty points, plus the A is on a double-letter score and the Z spot makes it a triple-word score, so I've got 93 points in one swoop."

"Well, I'll be damned."

Chapter One

Fifteen years later

Douglas MacLeod paused on the threshold of the workroom, disconcerted by the sight of a couple frozen in an intimate embrace.

No, not an embrace. It was more of a stance, Doug decided. A grapple. His lips curved in amusement. The man leaned over his lovely companion, his shirt pulled off one shoulder as if he were caught in the act of disrobing. The young woman was clutched against him, her back arching away from him, her long lovely throat bared to his lips.

It would have been a touching scene if there hadn't been papier-mâché rocks piled around them in a picturesquely haphazard fashion. Or if twin spotlights hadn't been set to highlight the couple.

Or if the woman's garb hadn't been quite so eclectic.

A torn sweatshirt was arranged to slide off her shoulder. A wide belt cinched a long flowing skirt tightly at her waist. The draping folds didn't disguise the fact that she wore jeans beneath it. And high-topped sneakers.

She was lovely despite the strange clothing, her nose pert, her jaw the least bit pointed. Her lashes were long and a deep rich shade of brown. Her long flowing hair was a pale blond and reached nearly to her hips as she arched backward.

"Bubblegum?" she grumbled from the side of her mouth. "God, Cliff. You know I hate the smell of bubblegum. Couldn't you chew Juicy Fruit? Or suck on a Certs?" Her eyes were only half open as if she were in the throes of a great passion rather than disgusted with the smell of her gallant's breath.

"I like bubblegum," Cliff defended himself. His sandy hair fell forward as if tousled. His lips hovered just above the sensitive area below her ear. "You should talk, Jan. What did you have for lunch? Liverwurst?"

"Very funny. You know very well it was peanut butter. You stole half my sandwich."

Fascinated by the asinine conversation as much as by the frozen tabloid they presented, Doug leaned against the molding around the door, his arms folded. He had come to Lloyd Amour Graphics looking for his old college buddy, and possibly even a temporary job. He hadn't counted on being entertained.

"Would you two shut up?" a third voice demanded from farther back in the room. Doug squinted into the dimmer regions of the place. He could barely discern the form of another man bent over a drawing board. He had an eyeshade on to protect his eyes from the glare of the lamp that arched over his slanted table. The sleeves of his blue work shirt were rolled up just below his elbows. "And suck in your gut, Cliff," the artist recommended. "What self-respecting hero has a beer belly?"

"This one," answered the man with the woman in his arms. "How much longer? Jan's put on weight since the last time you forced us to pose."

"Humph!" the woman snorted. "You've just turned into a couch potato since your divorce. If you just pumped some iron . . ."

"Or saw my chiropractor more regularly," he countered. "Honest, boss. My arm is giving out. I'm losing feeling in it."

The artist was apparently unaffected by the complaints. "Tilt your head back a little more, Jannie. I don't like the way this looks yet."

"Oh Lord," the posing man groaned.

"Wimp," the woman snapped and tilted her head as asked. The blond wig slipped off and slithered to the floor. Her own short brown curls sprang back into shape, clustering around her face.

"Hell," the man at the drawing board said. "Okay, take five, kids."

The couple straightened, breaking apart with visible relief. The man shrugged back into his shirt and hurried toward the back of the room. The woman swept up the wig and tossed it over the back of a chair. As she turned, she caught sight of Doug in the doorway.

"Hi," she said brightly. "You looking for Lloyd? He'll be back later."

Doug pushed away from the doorjamb. "Actually, I was looking for Jason Holloway."

"Too bad." She sighed. "I was hoping you were a model. We need one—actually, two—badly." She ran a practiced eye over him, noting the width of his shoulders beneath his striped dress shirt, and moving on to the cling of his comfortable old Levi 501s. Her eyes touched his dark hair, studied the faint lines at the corners of his eyes, lingered along the structure of his lips and jaw. "You're the type we need," she concluded. "Why not hang around and talk to Lloyd?"

Doug was a bit disconcerted when, after having sized him up, she dismissed him, and moved away to turn off the spotlights.

"Holloway," he repeated. "Could you direct me?"

"Over that way," she said with a nod of her head. The brown curls wiggled and settled back into place.

Doug looked at the way they clustered at her nape as she bent forward to adjust the angle of a rock-prop. He wondered if he would be able to taste that tempting spot if he stayed to pose with her in a frozen tabloid. It might make a brief stint as a male model almost worthwhile.

First things first though. He'd only been in town an hour and Jason Holloway was the reason he'd chosen Richmond, Indiana, over all other midwestern towns. Even from the glimpse he'd caught while wending his way to Lloyd Amour Graphics, Doug knew he had successfully escaped the big city.

Richmond wasn't sleepy but, thank goodness, it didn't look anything like a miniature New York City either.

The workroom at the graphics firm was more like a warehouse than an artist's work area. The man in the eyeshade was still bent over his table, his hand racing over his sketch, each stroke sure and bold.

Doug hadn't seen Jason Holloway since the day they'd taken a couple of six-packs of Strohs and a couple of equally intoxicating blondes back to their dingy apartment on graduation day. The next morning he'd been up and on his way to New York before Jase was awake.

They'd been roommates their last two years in college. Both art majors. Both with totally different concepts of what art should be. He'd been the conservative one, Doug thought. He'd actually been ecstatic to land a job with a New York City advertising firm. Jase had sneered at him and at commercial art in particular. Now, eight years later, they had each abandoned their original dreams. Doug had turned his back on the establishment, and it looked like Jason Holloway was now drawing commercialized covers for romance novels.

Despite the years, Doug recognized the quick movements of the artist in the eyeshade. He barely recognized his old roommate though.

For Jase the eight years had been hard and un-

17

kind. He was gaunt, not just in his face and long, gangly form, but in spirit. That much had come across in their brief phone conversation. The enthusiasm to make an artistic statement had been long in dying. It was sad, Doug thought. So much verve, so much energy, so much talent gone to waste.

All the time they'd been in classes together he and Jase had kept a friendly rivalry going. But it had been Holloway who had the real genius. Doug felt his own work was predictable. Jase found ways to twist things, to make them subtle but startling. Doug envied that dash. He had worked hard to find a spark of it in himself. But Jason's flame had always burned brightly.

Perhaps too brightly.

Doug stopped in front of the tilted drafting board and peered upside down at the hasty charcoal sketch. The strokes were fluid, the lines flowing to draw the eye toward the embracing couple, then moving downward toward the blocked letters of the title. Only there wasn't a title yet, just lines to indicate positioning.

The verve was still there. But the composition wasn't as copacetic as Doug thought it should be.

"Wrong clutch, Jase," he said. "Too predictable. You trying to emulate me?"

The man in the eyeshade glanced up. A smile split his face. "Doug!" He tossed both eyeshade and drawing charcoal aside. His faded blond hair hung limply to his shoulders. He looked like a shopworn Prince Valiant. His face aglow with pleasure, Jason leaped to his feet and threw his arms around Doug's shoulders.

Doug returned the bear hug with equal enthusiasm. "How the hell are you, Holloway?"

Jason stepped back. "Lord, not as good as you. Hell, look at you, MacLeod! You trying to bring us a touch of Park Avenue? What is that? A custom-made shirt?"

"Off the rack," Doug insisted. "Lord and Taylor's."

"Damn," Jason said. He fingered his own work shirt, liberally splotched with paint. "Off the rack, K-Mart."

Doug grinned. "It's good to see you, Jase."

"Yeah. Real good, MacLeod," the other man agreed with feeling.

" 'Course, you look like hell," Doug added. "Worse than usual."

Jason chuckled. "That's what bein' so damn popular does to a man. Come meet the crew."

Doug fell into step beside his old friend. "All freelancers?"

"Damn right. L'Amour's business fluctuates too much for Lloyd to keep a regular staff. Unless you can call us that. He always manages to lure four of us back here."

"L'Amour?"

"Pet name," Jason explained. "Lloyd's name lends itself well to our current project. Instead of designing containers and advertising for junk food or doing promotional posters for a local theatrical production this time, we're creating book covers

19

and the propaganda sheets for the sales staff of a small publisher. Firm's out of Indianapolis, planning on dipping into Middle America's pocketbook."

One corner of the room was arranged as a lunch area. A 12-cup Mr. Coffee sat on a scarred card table. The coffee hadn't been fresh for hours. A thin oil scum covered the surface. Around the carafe, a box of sugar cubes and a jar of powdered cream fought for space with a selection of abandoned mugs. Dilapidated folding metal chairs were pushed back from the table. There was a miniature refrigerator, the kind Doug had kept in his dorm room his freshman year, and a utility-sized stainless steel sink. Jars bristling with soaking paintbrushes were lined up on the counter nearby.

The man who had been stuck posing for Jason was reclining in a folding chair, his feet propped on a second. He hadn't bothered buttoning his shirt. Or sucking in his stomach. A can of Diet Dr Pepper stood at his elbow. A sheet of copy, fresh from the laser printer, was held near his face as he proofread it.

Jason kicked the second chair to get the man's attention. "This is Clifford Bogen," Holloway said. "Doug MacLeod."

Cliff looked up with a wide smile. "Ah, the New York contingent," he murmured. "Jase told us you were coming." Cliff set aside the proof sheet, careful to avoid the coffee rings on the table, and got to his feet. "How is the Big Apple?"

"Hectic," Doug said, shaking hands with Bogen.

He got a whiff of bubblegum as the man chuckled.

"Cliff is our copywriter," Jason explained.

"And part-time hunk," Cliff interjected.

From an adjacent alcove came the sound of a distinctively feminine snort. "Humph! Dreamer."

Jason stepped around the partition and leaned on the back of a bright blue office chair. The brunette with the short bouncy curls still had the long flowing skirt on, but it was bunched up around her hips and held out of the way between her thighs. The screen of a personal computer glowed on the desk before her. A variety of cute little pictures offered her a choice of windows in which to work. The little arrow of the mouse was aimed at the paintbrush. She hit the button to bring the screen up before turning to face the men.

"Janelle Ingraham," Jason introduced. "My college roommate, Douglas MacLeod."

She sighed. "Too bad. Not that it isn't nice to meet you, Doug," she said quickly and a bit contritely. "I was just hoping we were actually going to get some models for Jase to work with. I'm falling behind schedule on the promotion materials."

"Why worry?" Cliff asked. "Just work overtime and have Lloyd shower more money on you."

She glared at him. "It isn't money, it's time I need."

"Jannie does all our layouts," Jason explained. "From computer graphics to choosing the fonts for the print to the actual pasteups." He turned back to Doug. "Sorta like you did in Manhattan."

That caught her attention, Doug noticed. Her voice sounded carefully casual when she asked, "Are you any good?"

It was Cliff's turn to snort in derision. "He worked in New York City, Jannie. Of course he's good. He could paste circles around you."

There was suspicion in her look now, but the brunette kept her cool. "If only you could write copy, Doug," she drawled, "we could cut this poor sap free."

Holloway grinned at his cohorts, unconcerned with their sparring. Since Clifford hadn't taken offense, Doug figured the antagonism was all on the surface, part of the usual interplay of the pair.

"Children, children," Jason soothed, then turned back to Doug. "If you're interested, I could talk to old man Amour about putting you on for this project. We're rushing a deadline. The work is only temporary, though."

"That's because none of us can get along together on more than just a temporary basis," Jan added. "Artistic temperament."

"My ass," Cliff said.

Her brows rose in theatrical surprise. The sting of her tongue was still sharp though. "Yes, I thought that was where yours was, Bogen," she mused.

Jason drew Doug away from his associates' siblinglike squabble. "Our fourth member is Angie Vasco," Jason explained. "She does the typesetting and usually poses for me. But right in the middle of this project her boyfriend proposed. Angie's

22

dragging him to the altar before he can come to his senses. She's off making hurried arrangements. The wedding is this Saturday."

They ambled back to Jason's drawing board. Holloway waved Doug into the comfortable padded bar stool that served as his chair behind the board. Doug hooked his heels on the foot rail and leaned forward, forearms braced on his thighs. Jason dropped into a beanbag chair, his long legs stretched out, crossed at the ankles. He steepled his fingers before his face and stared up at his friend.

"So what's up?" Jason wanted to know.

Doug's mouth quirked in amusement. "I was going to ask you that."

"You mean—all this?" Jason waved a languid hand to indicate the warehouse atmosphere of Amour Graphics. "Sold out to the establishment so I could eat."

"Things were that bad?"

"Worse."

"If you'd accepted my offer to put you up and come to New York . . ."

Jason laughed. "Wouldn't have helped. I'd just have starved farther away from home. I'm one of Richmond's native sons, and here I stay. Now, what about you? I thought you had it made. Not only the job, but a fiancée."

"Chucked them both. She wanted me to be a great artist, someone with frequent showings in SoHo and the Village, and I didn't want to be in that kind of limelight."

"And the job?"

23

"Got to me. Couldn't take the pressure. Where the hell is the importance of a new and improved toothpaste when balanced against the homeless issue or events in the Middle East?"

Jason's grin widened. "Lord Almighty! You're a born-again liberal!"

"Please." Doug cringed. "I'm the first guy to turn tail at the sight of any political do-gooder."

At Jason's steady gaze, Doug shrugged. He ran a hand through his hair and leaned back in the chair. "Hell, just tired, I guess. Burned out. I saved a bit of money. Now I just want to enjoy life while I look for the meaning of it all."

"There's always the smaller art galleries," Jason said. "Or a stint here at L'Amour." He paused, his brow furrowed. "How much money have you hoarded away?"

Doug laughed. It felt good to be with Jason again. "Mercenary as ever when it comes to other people's money, I see."

"This is nothing like conning you into buying my art supplies," Jason insisted. "Amour's put this place on the market. He and his wife want to retire. The accounts are established. It would be a good investment. Especially for someone who knows the business."

"Like me?"

"Like all of us," Jason said. "We've all talked about it. Jan, Cliff, Angie. Me. But we're all too broke to even scrape together the down payment. I could mortgage the family abode, but that wouldn't come up with even a quarter of what we

24

need. Cliff's just coming out of a nasty divorce fight and his credit is shaky. Jan lives on what she makes as a freelancer and through the crafts market. Angie screens designs on T-shirts on the side. And her soon-to-be husband is a pressman at the newspaper. We're not exactly the type of clients the bank smiles on."

Doug took a deep breath. The money from selling his condominium wouldn't have bought him much in New York, but it could be stretched in Richmond. It was one of the reasons he'd decided to pack up and move there. The fact that Jason lived in Richmond had been the other drawing card. Why hadn't he remembered Jase could always find his way into another man's wallet?

Well, Doug had plans of his own. They were nebulous at the moment, only half formed. But buying a graphics company was definitely not part of his long-range scenario.

"I don't know, Jase," Doug temporized. "I only got into town. I need to find a place to stay . . ."

"I've got a drafty old place but you know you're welcome to stay as long as you want."

"I still need to settle into a new profession," Doug continued, hoping to make an impression on his friend. He hadn't come to take up their old relationship, one where he backed Jase up no matter what his own feelings were on a matter.

Jason glanced at his watch. It was a much abused Timex chronograph. The crystal and leather band were both spotted with tiny drops of paint. "So why dip into your funds? While you're thinking, help us out here at L'Amour. I know Lloyd will spring for another freelancer."

"Doing what?"

Jason grinned. He got up and stretched. "Yo, Jannie!" he called. "Show time. I've got you a new partner."

Chapter Two

Jan readjusted her long blond wig. This was absolutely nuts, she thought. Not only was she falling farther and farther behind in her own work, now she had to act enthralled and passionate with a complete stranger. It was tough enough doing it with Clifford whom she'd known forever.

It had been nearly three years since she'd opted for the frugal but free life of a freelance artist. After just a few assignments it was clear that she worked well with Cliff Bogen and Jason Holloway. They had become a team. When one of them landed a job, the others were quickly brought in. Angie Vasco had joined them this past year.

Opportunities for freelancers in Richmond, Indiana, were few. But then the competition for jobs was limited as well. Most graphics artists were looking for full-time positions. The kind with regular, decent-sized paychecks. Those with more luxurious tastes moved on to the larger cities—Dayton, Cincinnati, Columbus, and Akron, all over the state line in Ohio, or they headed west to Indianapolis.

Jan had worked in Indy. She hadn't cared for the dog-eat-dog competition in the city. Richmond suited her just fine. It was large enough to supply her subsistence income and still leave her sufficient hours to pursue her first love, crafts.

While her work as a graphics artist was praised by her peers, it was the decorator crafts she created in the off times that she found most satisfying. They were seasonally profitable, too. Just before the Christmas shopping season, she moved in with her parents in Indianapolis for a six-week stay. Their house was her headquarters while she maintained a small booth in one of the malls, selling decorated wreaths, quaint spoon dolls, sachets of potpourri, and dough ornaments. When she left Richmond each November, it was in a loaded U-Haul. Her stock usurped her parents' garage until the holiday season was over. Throughout the year she succumbed to the lure of various crafts shows, but the bulk of her inventory was saved for the mall booth.

It wasn't a lifestyle that appealed to her parents. They had hoped she would stay with an advertising agency in Indy, meet some nice man, get married and supply a horde of grandchildren. Jan had hated the advertising agency, and had yet to meet someone with whom she cared to spend her life. As an only child, she wasn't sure how she'd take to the procreation business. She was used to being alone.

Oh, there had been a man once who'd impressed her enough to share her roof for a brief period. A very brief period. That unsuccessful relationship had convinced Jan that she actually liked being alone.

Amour Graphics was the closest thing to a professional home that she had. The staff, both freelancers and the permanent employees, were as close as she got to family in Richmond. She was fond of Lloyd Amour and his perky wife, Sandy. Liked the flexibility they allowed the freelancers. Liked the generous wage Lloyd paid. The work wasn't frequent, but on her frugal budget a few weeks on assignment with L'Amour allowed her a couple of months of carefree crafts construction.

But she was an artist, not a model. She wished Angie hadn't gone off on this wedding tangent, sticking her with the unwelcome additional duty.

Damn! If Jason wanted models, why didn't he visit the local modeling agency and flatter some camera-struck teenager to play statue for him? Preferably one with a jock boyfriend who liked to play-act as well.

Such was not the case.

Jason sized up the setting once more. There was no backdrop of scenery. That he created like whole cloth from his imagination, giving the hills, fields, mountains, or forests a special otherworldly look. But his genius failed when it came to posing imaginary people. Particularly couples caught in the throes of passion. As if his reluctant models ever were, Jan thought in disgust.

She was posing for Jason only because she couldn't say no to someone who looked like a scrawny beggar with spaniel eyes. If he had been someone who survived on handouts, in truth, Holloway would have become rich at it. It was impossible to ever refuse him.

And he was a genius. His artwork made them all look good. Especially her layouts.

Jason was fidgeting, rearranging the papier-mâché boulders. He studied Jan a moment, then turned to Douglas MacLeod and insisted that he remove his shirt. The newcomer looked amused rather than startled at the request. He had a slow smile. It curved his lips as he unbuttoned his blue striped dress shirt and tossed it aside on a chair.

She had been right about his qualifications as a model for the cover. Doug's muscles were lightly developed, macho without putting him in the running for Mr. Universe. The deep brown curls that clustered on his chest were moderate. They dwindled into an interesting trail that led into the belt of his well-worn jeans. She liked the natural fall and auburn highlights of his thick dark hair. There was an amused gleam in his slate gray eyes when they met hers.

He really was a good-looking hunk. Perhaps grappling with this half-naked stranger wouldn't be so bad after all.

"This is nuts," MacLeod said, echoing Jan's earlier thoughts.

She moved into position before him. "You're telling me."

"Closer," Jase yelled from the shadows. "Hell, you saw what we're trying for, Doug. Put a little feeling into it."

The man from New York slid his arm around Jan's waist. "Nuts," he murmured again.

Jan stepped between his legs, put one hand on his naked shoulder. "You mean the situation or Jason?"

"Me," he said. "For doing this."

"Both of us," she corrected. "You've got to hold me a little tighter."

"Like this?" His arm drew her close against him. "Are we supposed to be reenacting a particular scene from the book?"

She liked the deep timbre of his voice, the slightly husky quality.

"Tighter. You've got to support my weight as I lean back," Jan directed. "I have no idea what happens in any of the novels. That's Cliff's area. Actually we're lucky to get the hair coloring right on the characters."

Doug readjusted his stance. "You don't read the story first?" His arm behind her back felt like steel. He didn't seem to be straining as Cliff had earlier in the same stance.

Jan tipped back experimentally. The long tresses of the blond wig rippled down her back. She checked the pins that held it in place, then the way her torn sweatshirt dipped off her shoulder. "Read? Who has time to read? The deadline doesn't allow for that luxury. Besides, for all I know, the writers are still hard at work. Cliff does

31

his blurbs from the synopsis. I don't know how they work it at the major New York houses, but our client is pretty small potatoes and wants the promotion material early in order to canvass bookstores. That means covers and copy, not completed novels."

"Closer," Jase yelled from his drawing board.

Doug's arm tightened, pulling Jan nearer, her pelvis smack against his. " 'Course, I could get to like this job," he mused.

Time to put the skids on this jock, Jan thought.

"Don't get any ideas," she growled, albeit half-heartedly. "We're just working." Of course work had never been like this before. Erotic and titillating. It was hard to remember she was merely posing with him. The stance wasn't quite right, though. "You need to be nibbling on my ear," Jan remembered.

His voice dropped to a new, more intimate level. "I thought you said not to get any ideas?" His breath against her skin was doing strange things to her. Jan felt warm and tingling. The warmth had nothing to do with the glare of the twin spotlights.

Jan fought the feeling, reminding herself that she hated posing for Jason like this. She had layouts to do, graphics to coordinate.

"At least you don't smell like bubblegum," she said. Actually, he smelled awfully good. She wondered what aftershave he used. It was a scent she was unfamiliar with. Probably some expensive stuff.

"You don't smell like either peanut butter or liverwurst, if it's any consolation," Doug said. "But I can't help wondering if you taste like them?"

Cheeky stranger. He was taking advantage of the enforced intimacy, knowing she had no control of the situation. Still he was Jason's friend. And awfully attractive.

Jan pulled herself together. "Kissing isn't in the script," she hissed.

His eyes dipped to her lips and lingered suggestively. "If I have to hold you like this much longer, it will be," he murmured.

Color flooded her cheeks at the mere idea. Her mouth felt dry at the thought. A far too pleasant thought. Jan licked her top lip nervously. "Listen," she began.

His eyes hadn't left her mouth. "Tempting," Doug mused. "But the spotlights could cramp my style a bit."

Jan glared at him. "You relieve my mind."

He grinned at her sarcasm. One eyebrow rose wickedly. "Let's see. What did you say was in the script?" His voice was an exotic rumble. "Something about nibbling on your ear?"

"Only looking like you are," Jan insisted.

"Spoilsport."

He was laughing at her now, Jan decided. And she was behaving like some damn tender virgin. Well, two could play this game. She'd show the big city hunk that this woman was a force to be reckoned with.

Back in the shadows, Jason swore. "I hate it. There's something wrong. No spark."

Jan took the opportunity to push out of Doug's arms. "You're supposed to invent the spark. Sparking is not in my contract."

MacLeod shrugged. "Don't look at me, I'm not even a bona fide employee yet." He rolled his shoulders as if the short time holding the stance had left them stiff.

Jan found herself staring at the way his tendons stretched with the casual movement. She needed someone to kick her, she thought. Imagine an intelligent, talented woman like herself being impressed by a macho display of male flesh!

"What's this book called?" Doug asked.

Jason ripped the sheet off his drawing board and crumpled it. "Don't ask me. Jan does the brochures. Which one is it, Jannie?"

She thought for a moment. "The rocks are probably the New Mexican setting. That means this one is for *Passion's Last Stand.*"

Doug choked down a laugh. "You're sure?"

"Certain," Jan declared. "Yo, Clifford! You wrote the blurb. What happens in *Passion's Last Stand?*"

The copywriter gathered up his pages of typeset material. The tails of his open shirt flapped as he crossed the room toward them. "Let's see," he said, his head bent scanning the sheet. "Here it is. 'Aphrodite Cartwright hated the half-breed Stark Savage for stealing her birthright. She vowed to

34

break him, but Stark had other plans. Plans that would make the lovely schoolmistress just one more thing he had taken from her father, Apollo Cartwright."

"Good Lord!" Doug said.

Cliff looked up with a grin. "I write what they give me to work with. No one said they were good novels. We're not talking a major publisher here."

"You can say that again," Doug breathed. "So I'm a half-breed named Stark Savage?"

"Could be worse," Jan pointed out. "I'm stuck with Aphrodite Cartwright!"

His smile could have been a smirk. She wanted to believe it was. But Doug's eyes weren't laughing. They were . . . thoughtful?

"The lovely schoolmarm and daughter of the apparently dastardly Apollo," Doug murmured then raised his voice. "Sharpen your charcoal, Jase."

Before Jan realized his intention, Doug had bent and swept her up in his arms. Cradled against his bare chest, she felt very strange. Almost vulnerable. What a disgusting state of affairs. Jan linked her wrists behind his neck. What was really disgusting was the realization that she liked the feel of his arms about her, one at her back, the other beneath her knees. The feel of his chest against her side. Liked it too damn much.

"And what, may I ask, are you planning?" she demanded.

Doug's grin was slow and intimate. There was a

new, disturbing singing in her blood now. Bad news.

"On getting out of here in under an hour," he said. "All it takes is giving Jase what he wants."

Jan forced her voice to be cool. "Gorilla seduces schoolmarm?"

The set of his lips was rakish. "And she loves it."

"Debatable," Jan growled. He was too sure of himself. Of his effect on her.

"Not for Aphrodite," Doug reminded her softly. "Just go with the flow, sugar."

Jan set her teeth, definitely suspicious now.

"You ready, Jase?" Doug called.

"Anytime." Holloway's voice echoed in the warehouse-sized room.

Doug's hold tightened. The trailing drapery of Jan's skirt swayed as he kicked the phony rocks out of his way. Then he dropped on one knee and placed Jan on the floor. The makeshift skirt swirled around her. Doug tilted her chin so that it gave Jason a smooth line. "What do you think, Jase?" he demanded. "Nice curve from Jan's lovely jaw down the arched length of her throat." The motion of his hand continued to skim lower, designating the rest of the pose, his fingertips hovering just above the gentle rise of her breast.

"What are you going to do?" Jan asked, not moving from her position.

"I'd say relax, but that's impossible," Doug allowed. "I think we can get this done quickly though if you lean back on one arm. The one toward Jase," Doug instructed. "Then curl your other arm around my neck."

His voice had altered to a more businesslike tone. Jan wondered if her earlier unease rose from the way her senses seemed heightened around him. They were just posing. Working.

"Fingers in your hair?" she suggested, determined to be as professional as he.

Doug grinned, the expression far more devilish than professional. "If the spirit so moves you, sugar," he murmured in that intimate tone again. His arm tightened around her waist and drew Jan up so that her back was arched. Their lips were just a breath apart now. A curiously weakening distance.

"Well, here goes nothing," Doug said and kissed her.

Jan jerked in surprise then went with the flow. This was acting, after all. No one had to know she was enjoying the curve this stranger was throwing. Of their own accord, her fingers tightened in his soft dark hair. Her lips parted naturally. As if he recognized the change in her response, Doug's mouth moved over Jan's with tender, but thorough force.

"Yowza!" Jason shouted. "That's it! Hold it! Breathe only if you must."

Jan doubted if she was breathing. She certainly didn't feel like an Aphrodite Cartwright, but something in her sure as hell was responding to Doug MacLeod's rendition of Stark Savage. Rather than think about how much she liked kissing a man she'd met barely an hour before, Jan tried to picture the way Jason's charcoal was racing over his page, catching their frozen pose.

"Got it!" Jason crowed. "Pure inspiration, MacLeod!"

Doug leaned back, a bit reluctantly, his arms still supporting Jan's weight. She blinked up into his amused gray eyes and gathered indignation like a cloak around her. So he thought it was funny that she'd fallen for his trick.

"I wouldn't call it inspiration exactly," she snarled.

"No? I've got tons of inspiration where you're concerned," he murmured, his voice as deceptive and deep as the purr of a caged panther. "Care to help unpack my etchings?"

He was laughing at her, teasing. But there was something other than simple amusement in his eyes. Something that warned Jan that Doug MacLeod was eminently male and damned dangerous.

Still a bit dazed, she found her fingers were still entangled in his hair. Hastily, she moved away from him. "I told you there was no kiss in the script."

He sat back on his haunches. "So I'm guilty of a little rewriting."

"Only a little?" Jan sneered.

Doug chuckled and got to his feet in one fluid move. He reached down to help Jan to her feet. "No hard feelings? Jase got what he wanted, so you're off the hook as a cover model now."

"True," Jan admitted.

"So why not show I'm forgiven," Doug suggested. "How about having dinner with me?"

Jan was a bit skeptical about his intentions. "Only dinner? You don't want to try out a few more ideas for Jason's edification?"

"It's tempting," he admitted, his lazy smile widening.

Damn! Why did men like him have to have such roguish grins? And why did she have to be such a ninny as to feel special when he flashed it at her.

"But for now I'll settle for food," Doug said. "Where's a good steak house?"

Chapter Three

Jan succumbed. It was perfectly logical, she told herself. She was making Jason's friend welcome. Her acceptance had nothing to do with her blood pressure. It had absolutely nothing to do with the way her body hummed or the fact that her common sense had abruptly deserted when Doug MacLeod kissed her.

As it turned out, dinner was not a quiet, intimate little meal for two. Jason and Cliff invited themselves along.

At least she looked extremely popular being the only woman at the table, Jan thought. Unfortunately for her ego, the men were practically ignoring her.

"So what's it like in the Big Apple?" Cliff demanded of Doug soon after their steaks were ordered. He was nearly finished with his first beer of the evening and had already ordered a second.

"Like anywhere else, only faster," Jason said. He looked to Doug for confirmation. "Right?"

MacLeod stretched back in his seat, one arm casually finding its way along the back of the bench behind Jan. Somehow she'd ended up sandwiched between him and Jason in the horse-shoe-shaped booth. Doug and Cliff held down the outside seats. While each of the men had bottles of beer before them, Jan was sipping a tall Coke Classic.

Doug laughed shortly at Jason's answer. "Thus speaks the voice of experience," he said. "How close did you get to New York the one time you decided to visit me, Jase?"

Holloway smiled wryly. "Columbus, Ohio. It was close enough."

Doug grinned at his old roommate. "Coward."

Determined not to be overlooked, Jan added her two bits. "So what did you do in Manhattan? Any special projects we might have seen?"

Doug's smile turned her way and softened slightly. Jan wished it hadn't. She still wasn't comfortable with the way she responded to the pull of that grin.

"Well, it wasn't book covers," he said. "Mostly annual reports for private companies. When the toothpaste pump came out we did a bit of pro-motional material for suppliers. Other than that it was basic things like mail order catalogs."

Cliff played with his empty bottle. "No gor-geous babes in bathing suits?"

"Only their photographs," Doug admitted. "We did a calendar or two."

Cliff brightened. "Now you're talking. It must have been great!"

"The calendar or the job?"

"Both."

"Oh, I don't know," Doug drawled and glanced at Jan. "I had a lot more fun today."

He probably expected her to blush, to flutter her lashes, Jan growled silently. To fall all over him. So what if she felt a slight tendency to do the latter? Physical attraction wasn't everything. She was proud that she'd managed to appear cool after that kiss. Doug MacLeod and the other men probably had no idea that she'd felt light-headed for nearly half an hour. She wasn't about to let them guess that a kiss had made her feel giddy. She didn't like admitting it to herself. Besides, as a rule, men seemed to have a high enough opinion of themselves without aid from her excitable pulse.

She certainly wasn't some inexperienced teen-ager, although it was hard to tell from the way her insides reacted to Doug. She just wasn't used to MacLeod's fast Manhattan pace, Jan told herself. In New York a man probably had to make an impression quickly or move on. Things were different in Indiana. Or she thought they were. Her own experience of man-woman things had been rather limited of late. If kisses like the one she'd been tricked into sharing with Doug were the norm in Richmond for couples who'd barely been introduced, she'd been living an awfully sheltered existence not to have heard of the new trend.

"So are we agreed that we go en masse to Angie's wedding?" Cliff asked. His second beer had arrived. He tipped it back, savoring the cool draft. "That way none of us has to look stupid for not having a date."

Jason took a pull on his own bottle. "Hell, you just want to look available in case Ange has a girlfriend who hasn't heard about you. Forget it, Bogen. Everyone in town knows you. Didn't your ex-wife buy billboards or something at all the main intersections during the divorce proceedings?"

"Did she ever do fliers to stick on the windshields of cars parked in all the major shopping centers?" Jan asked. "I volunteered to do the layouts for her."

"Vicious little cat. Don't get too close to her, Doug," Cliff warned. "She's got claws like a panther."

MacLeod arched his left eyebrow. Jan thought Stark Savage would look like that. Arrogant. Predatory. And, damn it, immensely amused. Did Douglas MacLeod take anything seriously? Well, she'd soon find out.

Lloyd Amour had returned to the office shortly after they had completed the rough layout for *Passion's Last Stand*. He hadn't been as enthusiastic about it as Jason, but admitted he was no judge of such work. He'd send Sandy in to look at it. His wife lived on a steady diet of romance novels. He had fallen in with Jason's suggestion that Doug be added to the payroll as another freelancer. In the morning Jan would be forced to rub shoulders with him at the worktable. He had turned down the offer to model for more covers, but agreed to help Jan catch up on the promotion layouts.

It wasn't a collaboration she was looking forward to. Her graphic design skills were among the best in Richmond. But how would they stack up against those of a man who'd held a job at a New York agency? Now that Doug MacLeod was in town, would she find fewer assignments came her way?

Not that she'd miss the type of work. Just because she was good at it didn't mean she preferred doing it. Still, it did keep her meager pantry stocked and a roof over her head for the best part of the year.

It was difficult to admit Doug's help would be appreciated. Especially when accepting it might hurt her income in the long run.

Worst of all, there was a part of her that looked forward to working in close quarters with him.

Secretly, Jan bemoaned the fact that they would not be collaborating as models for Jason again. Lloyd had also given in to Jason's demand for a couple to pose for him.

"So do we all go together?" Cliff asked Jan and Jason. "Or did you both scrape up dates for the wedding?"

Jan groaned. "You've got a one-track mind. You planning on catching the bouquet?"

"Garter," Clifford corrected. "Guys go for a little racier stuff, Jannie. Angie's garter will fuel my fantasy life nicely."

Jan opened her mouth to comment, caught a glance of the amusement in Doug's eyes, and shut it again. Fortunately, the arrival of their steaks made it appear she'd kept quiet because the waitress was present.

During the meal it would have felt unnatural to the freelancers if their conversation had not centered on the latest L'Amour project—the promotional fliers and covers for the local line of romance novels. Doug expressed interest in how the account had landed in Lloyd Amour's lap, and how detailed the various stages had been. But Jan and her associates weren't interested in how L'Amour got jobs, just in how much they were paid to do them.

While they talked, the food disappeared. Jason's spare form concealed an enormous appetite. He talked around his food, often accenting a point by stabbing his fork in the air. Although Clifford had written the copy and was just fine-tuning it, the actual foldout brochures would carry small reproductions of the covers. These were made to titillate the buyers at both the major warehousing centers and at individual bookstores. Jason had rough drafts that he worked from, quick charcoal sketches that he used as guides when he painted the cover in full color. Deciding the right palette was just as tricky as getting the right pose.

There was one point that all the freelancers were agreed upon. They were sure—well, pretty sure—that their covers and brochures would be better than the actual novels they were promoting. Doug laughed at the exaggerated modesty. They all had ego problems.

Just as he did, Doug admitted.

Right now it wasn't his abilities at a drawing board that had his ego smarting. It was his attraction to Janelle Ingraham.

He had never been a man who kept a well-stocked black book of beautiful women's phone numbers. He'd led a fairly monogamous existence, sustaining relationships for a number of months before moving on. It hadn't always been Doug who did the moving. Tina had left him.

Tina. His onetime fiancée. The woman who wanted brighter horizons than he could offer. Or than he *wanted* to offer.

When he was truly interested in something, Doug knew, he could be single-minded in pursuit of it. Like the job in New York City. Once it had seemed the highest goal, but when he achieved it, the reality left a dusty taste in his mouth. He'd hung in there, determined to prove his worth, determined to prove to himself that he was more than a small-town boy. Trouble was, you could take a kid out of Gary, Indiana, but you couldn't take Gary, Indiana, out of the kid.

Richmond might be nothing more than a stop along his way. Doug wasn't sure if he would return to Gary. His family had all scattered—his mother to LA, his father to Dallas, his sister to Washington, D.C. Perhaps he'd find yet another town that appealed to him. The only prerequisite was that he stay far from the lights of any big city.

Jason Holloway had brought him to Richmond, but if Doug stayed, there was a good chance that it would be Jan Ingraham who kept him there.

At least she would for a while.

Doug found he was very attracted to her. Was it the casual and far from sophisticated way she dressed? The blond wig and long skirt had been discarded back at L'Amour. Clad in well-worn jeans and sweatshirt, Jan was a far cry from the fashion plates he had worked with in New York. Rather than showing off her figure, Jan's outfit seemed to be disguising it.

In spite of that, she was damn sexy. Was it his weakness for bare shoulders that made him think so? Some men drooled over great legs. Others slavered over a woman's breasts or hips. But for him it had always been the elegant line of a collarbone, the gentle slope and curve of an arm. The exotic, casual droop of Jan's sweatshirt kept his thoughts returning to her.

He liked the way her short curls clustered around her ears and framed her face. Liked the way her blue eyes sparkled with enthusiasm over her work, or clouded with confusion. Like they had earlier when he'd held her in his arms. He had intended the kiss to be nothing more than a way to rile her. She'd dismissed him so quickly when he'd arrived at L'Amour. But it had become something more the moment his lips touched hers and Jan had responded.

Now he would be working with her. Become her trusted associate. Doug doubted she would be dissatisfied with his ability doing pasteups. He'd quit a job in New York only a few days ago, after all. He hadn't been fired. In fact, he'd been offered a promotion to stay. It hadn't even tempted him.

He might not know exactly where he was going just yet, Doug thought, but he certainly knew who he was going to go after during his stay in Richmond.

Jason speared the last bite of his steak and changed the conversation. As he had told Doug earlier, Amour Graphics was for sale. The idea was like a carrot before Jason's nose, something he couldn't ignore, couldn't reach, and couldn't forget.

He favored Jan with his hound dog expression. Big hungry eyes and a pitiful smile. "Think your parents would be willing to throw in with us on the down payment for L'Amour?"

Jan pushed back her half-eaten steak. "I asked. They sidestepped. I don't think we'll have any help there, Jase. How have your ideas panned out?"

He pointed to her plate with his fork. "You going to finish that?" Familiar with the plea, Jan traded dishes with him.

"I'm not doing much better," Jason offered. "I even hit Doug up."

"And?" Jan twisted in her seat to observe her new partner.

"And I did a fancy sidestep as well," Doug acknowledged. "Arthur Murray haunted me as a kid."

"Damn. It's so perfect for us." Jan sighed.

"For you and me, at least," Jason agreed. "Hell, with a little rearrangement at L'Amour there's room for a decent studio for me. I could paint on a much grander scale."

"I'd have more storage room for the crafts there. More space for the materials and a bigger workroom," Jan said.

Doug pushed back his plate, picked up his empty beer bottle and frowned at it. Where it had taken Clifford a good five minutes to get the waitress's attention, she rushed over to take their order as soon as Doug looked around.

"It doesn't sound like you two want to own a graphics business as much as you want to rent a warehouse," he observed.

Jan and Jason exchanged a glance. "But we know from experience that there are slow times. That's why Lloyd doesn't keep a regular staff, just a Rolodex of freelancers' phone numbers," Jason explained. "If Jan and I are set up for more than just graphics at L'Amour, we'll have less wasted time. When we finish an assignment, we can do what we'd prefer to be doing."

"Painting, huh?"

"In Jason's case but crafts in mine," Jan explained. "Heck, if I could expand, I'd be able to

49

supply gift shops. I've got a zillion business cards from interested parties."

Doug looked over at Cliff. "What about you? Lusting after L'Amour, too?"

Cliff toyed with his fresh beer bottle, smoothing his fingers down the condensation, drawing paths. "Yeah, it's a damn fever. It isn't like I need a lot of space like these guys," he said with a jerk of his thumb toward Jan and Jason. "But having a corner where I could do nothing but write would be great. Right now my typewriter is on a rickety card table in the corner of my bedroom. If things aren't going right on the script, it's too tempting to just chuck it for the day and take a nap or watch the boob tube."

He sighed. "The idea of having the computer to write drafts with rather than my beat-up old Smith Corona is an even better dream. I could do corrections, change things around. Print out one hell of a great-looking screenplay." Cliff took a long swallow of beer. "Do I lust after L'Amour? It might sound dumb, but I actually lie awake nights thinking about what a great opportunity this is. And how I can't afford to take advantage of it. Hell, I've even taken a mental inventory of relatives who might die and leave me something. Trouble is, no one has anything to will me."

Jan and Jason sighed in unison.

"Just our luck to come from families who are poor as church mice," Jason said.

"Yeah," Jan agreed. "Maybe I should have been more cooperative when I was in junior high

50

school and had a chance to butter up Great-Uncle Simon like Aunt Bea wanted me to."

"Old coot loaded?" Jason asked, his expression hopeful.

"According to Aunt Bea."

"Dead?" Cliff demanded.

Jan shrugged. The shoulder of her sweatshirt slipped a bit farther. Doug glanced at the other men and wondered how they could look so calm when merely sitting next to her was making him damn horny.

"For all I know, Uncle Simon's playing a harp now," Jan said. "I haven't been in touch with the far-flung fringe of the family in years. Besides, the only time I met him, we didn't exactly hit it off."

"Damn," Jason muttered.

Doug studied each of them in turn as they stared remorsefully into their drinks. A woman who wanted to expand her crafts output, an artist who craved a larger studio, and a hopeful screenplay writer in search of a niche. And Doug thought he was a dreamer!

Jan sighed again and finished her cola. "Did we ever decide if we were all going to Angie's wedding together?" she asked.

Doug welcomed the change of subject. The sooner the freelancers forgot about the sale of the graphics firm, the better. He'd learned to recognize disasters—especially after his short engagement to Tina—and the idea of these three buying Amour Graphics ranked right up there with the 1991 Super Bowl upset as far as he was concerned.

"I only have one question," he said, determined to lighten the atmosphere. "Do I get to tag along to the wedding reception? I hate to miss any chance to kiss a bride."

The drapes were drawn. The room air conditioner hummed. The three people at the foot of the large bed stared at the still form beneath the covers.

"I did all I could for him, Miss Ingraham," a blond young man said.

The middle-aged woman nodded sagely. Her dark hair was lightly streaked with gray and arranged in a gentle pageboy. Her blue eyes were slightly damp. She dabbed at her reddened nose with an embroidered handkerchief. Beatrice Ingraham had never cared much for disposable tissues. Even when she had a cold. Which she did now. There were no tears in her eyes for her dead uncle.

"You were wonderful, doctor," Beatrice soothed. "You kept Simon with us long enough for Walter to complete the new will."

"And you were an excellent witness that Simon was of sound mind when he made it," the other man said. "I was a bit surprised when Simon called me and indicated a change in the bequests. There may well be some squabbles when we probate it, but I don't see how anyone can dispute the will."

Beatrice touched his arm gently. "That's because you're a wonderful and thorough lawyer, Walter."

"And you and your niece Janelle are very fortunate women."

Beatrice looked at the now still face of the old man in the bed. "He looks peaceful."

"He should," the young doctor said. "He ran us ragged and enjoyed every minute of it."

"Simon liked to pull people's strings," Beatrice admitted.

"Well, he sure as hell pulled some doozies this time," the lawyer affirmed.

Chapter Four

The table was littered with scraps of paper, small reproductions of Jason's cover art, and sheets of copy in various type faces and sizes.

Doug stood on one side of the table glaring at Jan. She didn't appear concerned, but continued fiddling with minute adjustments to the brochure layout on the board.

He'd been working with her for more than a week now. Had been her escort to Angie Vasco's wedding. He'd been able to kiss the bride that day, but had yet to indulge his fantasies about Jan. And frankly, Doug admitted to himself, they were getting more vivid in his mind the more he rubbed shoulders with her.

He hadn't decided if she kept him at arm's length because she preferred not to mix business with pleasure, or whether she did so because she wasn't interested in him. Either way, the result was that Jan treated him the same as she did Jason and Cliff. Like she was his sister.

The idea galled Doug. It wasn't as if he were panting at her heels. Although he'd considered it the last two days. It wasn't as if she were cold either. He still remembered the sizzle of their posed kiss.

But he certainly wasn't getting any closer to trying another embrace. Not with a layout table between them. Jan was very careful to keep its full width a barricade to further "inspirations" on his part. Her casual indifference to his suggestions about the brochures hadn't helped ease the tension either. He was used to women fawning over his work. And him.

Doug frowned at the top of Jan's bent head as she worked. "I'm telling you that copy should be wraparound on the sales brochures," he insisted. Perhaps for the fourth time that day. "We've isolated the figures in that idiotic antique-looking frame, chosen the typeface for the title, even got the blurb about the author set. But you can't keep laying everything down in those neat columns, Jan."

From her position across the table, Jan favored him with a thin smile. Doug found it condescending. Which was unfair considering he was trying to improve the quality of their work.

"A bit of New York slap and dash?" she purred.

In the few days he'd worked with her, Doug had already come to know that tone of voice. There were times when he was sure she resented his aid. His recent past appeared to be a sore point. As if he could help it. So what if he *had* worked in New York City and she'd been content with small-town Indiana? Jan Ingraham was every bit as good as he was at this type of assignment.

And by now he knew that she disliked doing it as thoroughly as he did.

Jan wasn't the only thing that plagued him, though. The normal tempo of the days at Amour Graphics grated. It was too disconnected for a man used to things running on a well-regulated clock.

It took a damn miracle for the different parts of the project to come together at L'Amour. There was no set schedule. The freelancers drifted in as the spirit moved them. If Clifford didn't have the copy ready when Angie was there to input it, she took the rest of the day off. The same applied to Jan and Jason. Until Jason finished the final, full-color paintings to be reproduced, Jan couldn't complete her layouts.

Unfortunately, Jason's work habits hadn't changed in the years since Doug had last seen him. Holloway still felt more creative once the sun set, then he'd think nothing of putting in a straight fourteen hours of work, day after day without a break, if he was feeling inspired. It was par for the artistic temperament, but no way to run a business. During the week Doug spent as his old friend's house guest, he had tried to force a little more professionalism into the graphics firm. He had dragged Jason out of bed, poured coffee down his throat, and driven him to Amour by nine. As a result, all but two of the covers were complete.

Although Jason and he had once been in complete sync as to living arrangements, it had been a long time since Doug had shared quarters with anyone but Tina. Within forty-eight hours Doug was anxious to find a place of his own and, not only set up his own home studio, but get moving on fulfilling the dream that had sent him high-tailing it out of New York. It didn't take more than one morning to locate an apartment. Doug had his criteria. It had to have a large tiled area for his studio, since sculpting with clay was often messy. But it also had to be within a very short distance from Jan Ingraham's place. Doug had set a few sights, and his graphics partner was dead center on the current target.

Once Doug moved into his own apartment, Jason reverted to his usual habits, showing up at the graphics studio long after the sun had reached its zenith. At least his earlier efforts had provided materials, and black and white photostats of the four finished covers, enabling the layouts to move forward.

Or they would have, Doug reminded himself, if Janelle hadn't suffered from the same syndrome as Jason.

It wasn't as much of a pain to drive to her place each morning, though. Doug liked the old farmhouse where she lived. There were few amenities but the charm of the deep porch that wrapped around the two-story white clapboard house outweighed the lack of air conditioning. He liked the folk art look that dominated her decorating, too. A brightly colored patchwork quilt was the focal point in the front room, complemented by a rag rug in rainbow hues. There was a long sofa draped with crocheted afghans and piles of floor pillows for seating. Baskets were everywhere, spilling over with an assortment of dried flowers, ribbons, fabric, wire, and the other materials she used for her crafts. A roughly sanded and naturally stained hutch displayed speckled blue china and barn red pottery mugs. He'd never seen the top of her dining room table. It was covered with more craft materials. Drying grapevine wreaths hung on the ladderback chairs around it.

The place would never make a layout in *House and Garden* magazine, but it was definitely homey.

And it suited Jan.

It appealed to Doug, too. Especially that pile of pillows on the floor. He'd been dreaming about how Jan would look sprawled against them, her arms welcoming, her eyes cloudy with passion, her lips glistening and waiting.

He hoped that it wasn't a combination of his fantasies and his own plan for the future that made her so attractive to him. She appeared to fit both so well. *Take things slow,* he counseled himself. *You jumped with Tina and look where it nearly landed you. Don't make the same mistake again.*

Easier to give himself the good advice than to actually take it. Especially when Jan seemed so damn wholesome each morning when he picked her up. Her fresh scrubbed face, natural curls, and unconscious grace only made it harder to keep the distance she seemed to impose.

Although she was always awake and dressed when he arrived, Jan did have a tendency to dawdle over her morning coffee. Telling himself it was the deadlines that drove him, Doug had practically dragged her out the door the first couple of days. That morning, he'd been pleasantly surprised when she'd been waiting on the porch for him.

The pleasure he felt in her company had not diminished as he got to know her better. At times Jan seemed to reciprocate his feelings. At others, she held him at arm's length with those irritating sisterly mannerisms. But with either Cliff, Jason, or the newly married Angie always around at L'Amour, he had little chance to take their friendship into more intimate territory. He'd hoped that by getting his own apartment and casually inviting her for dinner, things would progress. Jan had surprised him by declining the invitation.

The way she'd been responding to his suggestions about the layouts didn't bode well for any change in their relationship in the near future either. It was a depressing situation that made him prickly over her comments about his work.

Doug watched as, across the table from him, Jan tested various Victorian border treatments around the tiny stat rendition of one of Jason's cover designs. The cling of her white jersey kept her shoulders covered but far from hidden from his lusting gaze. The low scoop neckline still offered a wonderful view of her elegantly shaped collarbone. The fabric gaped slightly away from her breasts as she leaned over her work. A long necklace of blue-tinged corn kernels dangled between her breasts. Their hue matched the cornflower swirls in her long sweeping georgette skirt.

Fleetingly, he wished he had an excuse to sweep her into his arms as he'd managed that first day. But posing for one of the covers wasn't actually what he had in mind. And the workroom at Amour Graphics wasn't the right place.

Irritated at the hopelessly single track his thoughts continued to travel, Doug glared at the layouts spread on the table. "What has my working in New York got to do with it?" he demanded. "I'm talking what's right for this project."

Jan was in complete agreement with his suggestion. The sales brochures would be more distinctive with wraparound copy. But that wasn't what Penn Publishing wanted. They had contracted with Amour because Lloyd had promised to give them full artistic control. She doubted Doug would understand that. In New York clients probably trusted the agencies to create what was best and didn't dictate what was to be done. Or at least she supposed they did. Things didn't operate that way at L'Amour.

They would if she owned it. But Lloyd put money before creativity.

"Humph," she mumbled. Since there was nothing she could do about it, Jan was immune to Doug's tirade. She chose a simple design of morning glory tendrils to use as a frame around the cover stat she'd been working on and fitted it.

The miniature rendition of Jason's painting showed the forms of a ghostly man and a very endowed mortal woman grappling intimately. The simple script letters she'd chosen for the title were emblazoned across the lower third of the page. *Spirit in the Sheets*. Cliff had tried to write up the back cover blurb as "an erotic romp with ectoplasm." Although probably very apt, his suggestion had been hooted down by the others.

"It doesn't matter what you or I think would look good," Jan said, her head still bent over her work. "It's what the big shots at Penn Publishing think. They were very specific about things. Even these stupid frames are their idea." She rubbed a smidgin of rubber cement from one corner of the layout.

The calm tone of her voice defused his frustration. A bit.

Doug leaned on his fists, staring at the layout upside down. His own work had centered around a glitz novel of the beverage business entitled *Lemon, Lime and Lust.* He wondered if the people at Penn Publishing were really serious about this line of romance stories.

"They'd all look better if we used the same frame around each cover illustration," he said.

"You know that and I know that," Jan agreed. "Continuity is not something the forces-that-be understand though. I like the art nouveau look you did around *Lust.*"

Her compliment surprised him, gave him hope. He shrugged it off, nonchalantly. "It went with the bubbles in the bottle," Doug conceded. He did know that Jason had detested that particular cover. It showed the silhouette of an amorous couple inside a tall spring-green soda bottle. It was odds-on which beverage company would take exception to the cover. Then again, it was doubtful any of them would ever see it. The more that Doug learned about the Penn Publishing titles, the less he considered them a threat to anyone. With distribution limited to the midwest, and probably nonexistent with the big chain bookstores, he doubted if anyone would ever see them.

"Shouldn't you have saved that vine design for *The Femme Fatale Farmer?*" he suggested. The blurb for Aphrodite and Stark's tome had been bad enough. But they were all afraid to read what Clifford had written about *Femme.* He'd nearly strangled while drafting the copy for it. He hadn't been able to stop laughing.

Jan straightened up and rubbed at the crick in her neck. "You could be right. What else have we got to do?"

She was still being all business. But the usual wall of reserve didn't seem quite as high. Doug decided to play along. Watch for his moment. He swore he wouldn't miss the first sign Jan gave that she'd welcome more personal attention.

"Two others yet," he answered and picked up a sheet of Cliff's copy. "The one Jase is working on now. *Literary Liaisons*—lust in the stacks at the New York main library. Can't picture it myself. And the last one, the return of Stark and Aphrodite in *Passion's Final Frontier*."

Jan groaned just at the thought and used both hands to massage her neck. "I wonder if the authors are actually using their own names on these things? I'd be embarrassed to have anyone know I wrote this trash."

"Oh, I don't know," Doug mused. He held up the larger stat of *Passion's Last Stand,* the cover that he and Jan had been roped into posing for. "Think anyone will recognize you in the blond wig?"

Jan pushed their mechanicals aside and scooted up onto the table. She leaned toward Doug to get a better look at Jason's drawing. She hoped that no one she knew recognized her. Even though they'd actually been kissing, Jason had drawn the characters as if they were a breath away from the type of mindlessly bruising kiss she and Doug had shared. She had no trouble recognizing her own profile, though. Or Doug's.

"You know anyone around these parts, Manhattan?" Jan asked him. Her voice was a low growl, almost a purr. "You might never live this down, you know."

The sound of her voice curled around him. She was still keeping distance between them. Doug could tell it in the way she snarled the word *Manhattan,* as if she hoped to annoy him with it.

Doug decided to put things into his own court. He dropped the stat back on the table. As if of its own volition, his hand slid into the curls at the nape of Jan's neck and pulled her nearer. His lips curved in a roguish grin. "I don't regret posing that afternoon," he said quietly. "In fact, I've been looking for a chance to repeat it."

He was pleased when she didn't pull away. "Like posing for the last cover? Reprising Stark?" Jan murmured. She leaned closer, her weight braced on her hands against the tabletop.

Not sure how far to tempt fate, Doug let his eyes dip to her lips briefly. "I can do without the playacting this time."

Jan was sure he could hear the way her heart quickened at his touch. She'd been waiting for a week for him to make a move. When Doug had kept his distance, she'd begun to think she'd imagined the spark that had passed between them.

She had certainly misjudged him that first day. The kiss had been nothing more than acting after all. Something that Doug MacLeod apparently excelled at and she didn't. She had thought he was interested in her when he began picking her up each morning. In the hopes that he would invite her out again, Jan had dawdled at home in the mornings, giving him plenty of time to suggest dinner or a movie. It had been just her luck that the one time he had asked her out, she'd agreed to drive to Indianapolis for her great-uncle's funeral that night. After a brief token appearance, Jan had headed back to Richmond. She didn't mention the circumstances of her trip to anyone at L'Amour in the event that Jason scented a nonexistent inheritance in the wind. It had been bad enough listening to the other relatives second-guess what Simon's will would leave them.

Fleetingly, Jan hoped that in the far corner of the room Jason stayed engrossed at his easel. With her lips so close to Doug's, and her body arched submissively toward his, she was afraid Jason would decide they were enacting the perfect cover once more. And she didn't want an audience the next time Doug kissed her.

There had been little else that she'd thought about over the last few days. When she was at L'Amour it was difficult to concentrate on the layouts with him so near. At night, it was nearly impossible to sleep for thinking about him, and the wonderful sensations of that very public kiss. Yet he was so businesslike when he picked her up. She had thought his only intention was to keep everyone's nose to the grindstone. Something none of them was used to doing. Part of the joy of working for Lloyd Amour was his hands-off management. He set a deadline, and when they didn't make it, despite talking as if it were foremost on their minds, Lloyd simply set a new one. Since he always called the same freelancers back, Jan had a sneaking suspicion that Lloyd never told them the true deadline. He simply adjusted schedules to their own natural rhythms.

Being fresh from the pressures of the big city, Doug didn't understand the system. From the expression she'd caught on his face since joining the L'Amour team, their casual habits would drive him crazy if he stayed in Richmond and became part of their group. Jan doubted he would. There was still too much of New York in Doug's makeup for him to be content with freelancing with them for long. He'd branch out on his own. If he stayed. She had little hope of that either. The thing to do was just enjoy the time they had together. It had begun to look like their friendship would be the same type she had with Jason and Clifford.

Or almost the same. Jan had a feeling that she

and Doug could never be only friends. She certainly was haunted by the memory of that searing kiss they'd shared. Was Doug?

The touch of his fingers in her hair was extremely pleasant. She closed her eyes, savoring the moment, hoping that he would take the hint and kiss her again.

As if he read her thoughts, Doug drew her closer. Jan could feel the soft caress of his breath against her cheek, felt it move nearer her waiting mouth.

She sighed softly in anticipation. Parted her lips.

And jolted upright, out of his reach, when the swinging double doors from the front office flew open with a crash.

Damn, Jan and Doug thought in unison.

"Where is that marvelously talented man?" the woman in the archway demanded brightly. Her gaze moved around the room, rested on Doug, and gleamed even brighter. "My God!" she breathed in awe. "You're Stark Savage!"

Jan slid off the table and glanced over at her partner. He had straightened and shoved his hands in the pockets of his jeans. The expression on his face seemed distinctly uncomfortable.

The stranger advanced, her stride long and athletic, the skirt of her pale pink chiffon tea-dress flowing behind her, her matching pumps clicking on the cement floor. A pert little shepherdess hat with a bobbing white plume sat rakishly on her shoulder-length blond hair. Lloyd Amour trailed in the visitor's wake, his balding pate, plump form and helpless expression making him seem like a lackey rather than the owner of his own graphics firm.

The woman sailed up to Doug and walked around him, her eyes moving over his tall, muscular form. Her eyes lingered over the way his dress shirt stretched across his shoulders, and, from behind his back, admired the snug fit of his acid-washed designer jeans.

She tossed back her pale hair. Her green eyes sparkled like faceted emeralds. "Yes, yes," she murmured. "I couldn't have chosen a more perfect specimen myself." Then she whirled around and accosted Lloyd. "So where is he? This genius who did the covers?"

She patted Doug's arm as if comforting him. "You're very nice, of course, dear, but I've come all this way to meet the artist. Perhaps later."

While Jan stood there stunned, Lloyd tried to make introductions. "This is Ms. Charlotte Penn, of Penn Publishing," he explained. "This project of ours is her brainchild."

Charlotte simpered. She was a young woman, perhaps thirty at the most, Jan guessed. And pretty. If you liked that rich, perfect complexion and the expensive, casually worn attire. Terribly conscious of her own tousled curls and far from fashionable clothing, Jan tried to be cool in her greeting.

The newcomer didn't even notice.

"The romances are very dear to my heart," Charlotte murmured modestly. "I've always wanted to be a writer but never liked the lack of control an author has over the way her books are marketed at the large publishing houses. So my father decided to purchase our own publishing company."

Jan translated that as meaning the flamboyant Ms. Penn's father was overly indulgent. When Charlotte had tired of all the rejection slips from the major publishers, she'd simply flattered her father into getting her into print. If the titles and Cliff's blurbs were anything to go on, Jan thought, the editors in New York had shown excellent taste in rejecting Charlotte's manuscripts.

"It was very difficult to decide exactly what type of story suited my style best," the pampered rich woman continued. She was oblivious to the fact that none of her three listeners had shown the slightest interest in her artistic struggles.

Doug hitched his hip against the edge of the table. "So you wrote all of the titles?"

Charlotte beamed at him. "Ohhh," she said, her eyes half closing. "Even the voice is right. Have you ever considered becoming an actor? When we do the screen version of *Passion's Last Stand,* you would be the perfect man to play Stark."

When Doug hastily declined the honor, Charlotte swept her smile over Jan then returned her gaze to Doug. "To answer your question, yes, I wrote all six of the stories. Of course I had to use phony names on them. But we prolific writers have to descend to such complicity so that we don't flood the market, you understand. A select few know that I'm Penelope L. Charles, Astrid Charlevoix, and Lotta Peters. My father suggested that I not use my own name on any of them, because of the publishing house name."

Clever man, Jan thought. And diplomatic. He'd probably had to read his daughter's output and hadn't wanted anyone else to know she lacked talent.

"Once these first titles hit the stands, we can leak the truth to the press," Charlotte bubbled on. "After all, everyone knows that Victoria Holt is really Jean Plaidy, and that she also writes as Philippa Carr."

Jan commiserated silently with the unaware Ms. Plaidy for having so inspired Charlotte Penn.

"Naturally, my style is nothing like hers," the inept author declared with a touch of modesty. "I believe I've found a more enduring style."

Jan nearly choked. Fighting down her laughter, she murmured, "Something in a more literary vein?"

Charlotte upped the voltage of her smile. "Literature! Absolutely! You understand exactly, Miss—well, I've forgotten your name. You look familiar, though. Oh, I have it. The hair is wrong, but you played Aphrodite, didn't you."

She glanced aside at Doug, measured him quickly, and went back to Jan. "I see! You and Stark—"

"Doug."

"Whatever. It was that chemistry between you that made the cover so memorable!" Charlotte declared. "Well, I'll keep my hands off him, dear Aphrodite. After all," she swept around to the silent, and rather stunned, Lloyd Amour. The plume in her hat bounced. "I didn't drive all this way to meet you. It was the artist I wanted to congratulate in person."

With barely a second glance at Jan and Doug, Charlotte spun around and strode to the center of the room. Moments later she was falling all over Jason Holloway with yet more cries of delight.

Chapter Five

The day had gone to the dogs after the arrival of Charlotte Penn. At least it had as far as Jan was concerned.

The budding intimacy between herself and Doug had vanished like a puff of smoke. Charlotte had dominated the premises at L'Amour, demanding to be told and shown each step of the production process. Jan was sick to death of hearing Lloyd explain four-color processing, of Jason's voice describing brush stroke and texture. Even Clifford had been hanging on Charlotte's every word once he learned she was spearheading movie versions of her books. Jan could almost picture dreams of doing the screenplays dancing in his head.

She and Doug tried to continue their work, but the constant interruptions, and Charlotte's breath at their shoulders, had not been conducive to productivity. At three o'clock they gave up and became part of Charlotte's audience.

Jan sustained herself with hopes that, when he

took her home, Doug would take up where they'd been interrupted. He hadn't. He'd been thoughtful, distracted when he'd driven her back. With the mood broken, they returned to being professional with each other, speaking only of the design jobs still to be done.

Jan was becoming thoroughly sick of dealing with the layouts for Penn Publishing.

Her spirits sinking, Jan stood inside the screen door of her rented house and watched Doug's car pull away. Well, what did she expect? She wasn't gorgeous like the women he'd probably known in New York. She was a real hick in comparison. Her wardrobe was comfortable rather than stylish. Her makeup was minimal, her nails were short. She might have a degree in commercial art but she was far from knowledgeable about the arts. She knew what she liked. Recognized the old masters from art history classes. But she was ignorant when it came to discussing the painters who dominated the modern art scene.

Doug probably knew them all. Had probably attended gallery openings, hobnobbed with the shooting stars.

Jan went into the living room and collapsed on the sofa. She stared across the room at the one painting on her wall. Jason had done it, an ethereal forest of soft pastel shades. She'd thought it the perfect setting for a unicorn, but Jason had been appalled at what he called her "poster" taste.

Well, she'd known back in school that she

wasn't a great artist, would never be one. She liked sketching, dabbling in paint. It was working with her hands that appealed more to Jan. She'd taken to clay modeling with a passion but had never managed to get her subjects looking the way she wanted. Her composition was always good, her teachers said. She was competent. But she wasn't brilliant. Not like Jason. Not like she figured Doug was. He had to be good. He'd landed a job in New York City.

Crafts were her forte. Her natural sense of composition was a plus when it came to arranging dried flowers artistically against rustic wreaths. The entwined grapevines, bound straw, and other natural materials she used were extremely popular. Bedecking them with flowers that she gathered and dried, made them unique.

It was when Jan was surrounded by her "weeds," that her creativity came to the forefront. Because they were unlike the commercially produced arrangements, her creations were in demand at decorator stores in the Richmond area. She'd received calls from shops in Dayton and Indianapolis as well and had supplied them with limited selections. None of the commissions was enough to live on. But she thought a few more steady accounts could make the difference, if only she could expand. That was the key.

If only, Jan thought again with longing.

She never carried the dream much further than those two words.

Now it was beginning to look as if Doug

MacLeod was going to slip into one of those "if" categories.

Jan heaved a sigh and pushed thoughts of L'Amour, the brochure layouts, and, most particularly, Doug, from her mind. A list of things to do lay on the dining room table awaiting her attention. Jan picked it up, musing over the various items for her consideration.

Wreaths. She glanced at the stack of waiting grapevines overflowing a large basket in the corner. Naw. Not in the mood. It was a big job to soak and then mold them as she wanted. Better to put it off until after the L'Amour assignment ended.

Next on the list was to collect wildflowers.

Jan looked out the window. It might be June, but there wasn't enough daylight left to do that. She had made friends with a number of rural families whose farmsteads still had spots of untouched forest land. Collecting and drying her own materials cut down on costs considerably. It was one of the pluses of living in a small town. The countryside was still in cultivation, and the sides of the back roads were often filled with brilliant blooming weeds.

What were weeds to others, Jan saw as perfect natural additions to her arrangements.

The old farmhouse she rented on the outskirts of Richmond was perfect for her needs. She had loved the Victorian look of the place when she first saw it. Two-storied with the wide porch wrapping along two sides, it represented the less frantic lifestyle of another time. Jan had added a porch swing and pots of African violets along the ancient veranda. Often she worked outside in the summer evenings, enjoying the long hours of dusk, watching the fireflies flicker, listening to the birds end their days in excited chirping.

Upstairs one whole room was devoted to drying bits of nature. Cattails, milkweed pots, and yarrow were frequently used in her arrangements. But Jan's favorites were the more colorful plants—purple larkspur, yellow Saint-John's-wort and creeping lady's-sorrel, bright orange butterfly weed, brilliant lady's thumb, Deptford pinks, and wild columbine. They were all sprayed and hung to dry, awaiting their turn in Jan's arrangements. She had also collected interesting stones from streams, often with lacy fossil designs prominently displayed, and twisted bits of weathered wood. In her rambles through the tiny copses she'd even found where a pioneer had carved his initials and a date into the bark of a tree. The year had been 1794.

Today wasn't the day to play forest sprite, though. Jan scanned her list, quickly squelching the idea of doing needlework or painting faces on wooden spoon dolls. No, she needed something that would work out her frustrations. Something a little more strenuous.

Jan let the list float back to the table and moved into the kitchen. A quick check of the cupboards showed she had more than enough flour. Beating, rolling, and shaping dough ornaments for the Christmas booth would suit her mood. It might even have an added bonus. With a decent addition to her stock she would wangle her way into the Starving Artists Show in Miamisburg over the Ohio line early in the fall.

She dropped a Glenn Frey cassette into the stereo and cranked up the volume. While the former member of the Eagles crooned about true love, Jan pummeled the dough into shape and sang along.

The first batch of Santa's helpers had been formed and were resting on the cookie tray when the phone rang.

"Pizza or fried chicken," Jason demanded when she answered. "I'm buying."

A little disappointed that her caller hadn't been Doug, Jan crooked the receiver between her ear and shoulder and continued working on the elves. "You?" she murmured.

Jason ignored the exaggerated disbelief in her voice. "Better get over here before the guys from the nuthouse take me away, Jannie."

Jan looked at the neat lines of jolly little dwarfs on her cookie tray, and listened to the tick of her ancient gas oven as it maintained the desired heat. She sighed. "Can't. Knee-deep in ornaments." Jason knew what that entailed. She'd dragged him into "cookie" duty the year before when she was running late.

"No problem," he declared. "We'll bring it to you. You got any beer?"

"Keg's empty." She only bought a six-pack

when company was expected. "I've got a fresh jar of sun tea," she added helpfully.

Jason made a gagging noise. He hated her tea. "We'll bring the beer, too," he said. "Be there in half an hour or so."

It took longer. Jan was just sliding her first batch out of the oven when the food arrived. She had expected to see Clifford, and even the recently married Angie in Jason's wake. For so long the four of them had done everything together. But when Jason barreled through her door and plopped the bucket of Kentucky Fried on her hastily cleared kitchen table, Doug was the only addition to their makeshift party.

Her heart did a funny little somersault when he grinned at her and made himself at home, yanking open the refrigerator door to deposit a twelve-pack of beer inside.

"What's this all about, Manhattan?" she muttered. "We celebrating something?"

Doug pulled three bottles of Strohs out, his fingers weaving around the narrow necks. "Search me," he said as he straightened up. "Jase is riding on some kind of adrenaline though."

Jason clucked his tongue against the roof of his mouth. He opened the container of chicken. The heavenly smell mingled with that of cooking dough. "You two are so suspicious," Jason stated. "You got plates, Jannie?"

Jan opened a cupboard door and passed dinnerware out. "We know you too well. The world's foremost freeloader. If you're buying,

Jase, there has got to be a catch."

He looked pained but his eyes were dancing with excitement. Once they were seated, he passed the container of coleslaw around and distributed biscuits. "Can't a man treat his two best friends once in a while?"

Doug nearly choked on his beer. "Once? Hell, I've known you for nearly ten years. This is the first time you've ever bought me a meal."

Jan spread honey on a biscuit. "So who do we have to kill?" she wondered.

Jason leaned back and beamed at them. "The fates have smiled on us," he announced. "L' Amour can be ours for the asking."

Doug savored another gulp of beer before asking. "Win the lottery?"

Jan hastily swallowed a mouthful of chicken and licked her fingers. "What are you talking about? I thought we'd gone over that. There is no way we can come up with enough for even a down payment. Even if we found a bank stupid enough to risk a loan on us."

"We're not talking about a bank," Jason declared. "We're talking about a windfall."

Jan and Doug stared at him.

Jason finished off a chicken leg before explaining. "You see, Charlotte Penn is enthralled with my paintings. She wants the original acrylics for each of the covers framed for her home."

Jan reached for her bottle of lager and poured it into a glass. As the foam rose, she kept her eyes on it rather than have to dwell on the flushed excitement in her deluded friend's face. Poor sap, she thought. Jason had waited so long to be recognized, he was willing to jump at any enthusiastic patron.

"Well, you've got enough finished canvases stockpiled to sell her," Jan admitted. "But I don't know if that'll be enough to buy L'Amour."

Doug was very familiar with his friend's output. He'd had to weave his way around the canvases while staying at Jason's. The Holloway homestead was Jason's private warehouse. Finished works lined the hallways, and were propped against nearly every vertical surface in the place.

"Even if Charlotte bought the lot, it wouldn't be enough to cover a down payment, Jase," he pointed out. "I know you never ask for more than a couple hundred a shot. Now if you're planning on hitting our eccentric debutante for a couple grand each, then. . . ."

"You don't get it," Jason insisted. He grinned widely at his friends. "I'm not selling my stuff to her. I'm saying we point out the possibilities at L'Amour to her and have Charlotte buy the place herself."

Suddenly the Colonel's recipe wasn't sitting too well on Jan's stomach. "You're nuts. Crackers."

"Charlotte won't do it," Doug said. "It's her old man's money, not hers."

Jason tipped his beer bottle, pointing the neck at them. "Oh, I know that. And he'll be careful with his loot. But if Lotty wants something, he usually gives it to her."

Jan and Doug exchanged a look. "Lotty?" Jan asked.

"She told me to call her that," Jason admitted modestly.

"Damn," Doug breathed as a new and horrible idea occurred to him. "You're planning to romance her into it, aren't you?"

Jason cleared his throat and looked uncomfortable.

Doug was feeling ruthless though. "Jase?"

Jason shrugged, trying to appear unconcerned. His eyes had a distant, almost dreamy look.

Jan pushed her plate aside. "Damn it," she growled. "You aren't really going to kiss up to Charlotte Penn. She'd lord it over us, Jase. You see how she is about these covers. Things have to be her way. It doesn't matter if that way is wrong." Frustrated anew, Jan hid her face in her glass of beer. A little puff of foam clung to the tip of her nose.

Doug took up the argument. "Charlotte may like your current covers, but what about others? She's too opinionated, Jase. And you're too undisciplined. It sounds like a good idea to you now, but what about when she loses interest. What about when her father wants profits, not paintings? What about—"

"What about giving the idea a chance?" Jason demanded. He pushed away from the table and stood up, glaring at them. "Hell. What's the matter with you two? I thought you'd like the idea."

He turned to Jan. "Especially you," Jason

said. "It's our one chance, Jannie. Can't you see that? Lotty and her dad live in Indy, not here. They'll be willing to leave things in our hands. We'll have free rein. I know it."

Jan concentrated on her glass. Her fingers slid back and forth in the condensation on the sides. "You're dreaming, Jase. It won't be that way. If they were that type, they wouldn't be keeping as close an eye on things. Just the fact that Charlotte showed up here today . . ."

"But she didn't come to check on things," Jason insisted. "She came because she fell in love with the photographs of the covers. She wanted to see them in person. Wanted to meet me."

Definitely deluded, the poor sap, Jan thought. "Jase. Think about it. Just from my standpoint, if nothing else. If she really was the hands-off kind of employer, she wouldn't be insisting that the brochures have that textbook look to them. To make them effective sales tools, the copy should wrap around the reproductions of the covers. They shouldn't have those dumb frames. They—"

Jason ran his hands through his hair until it stood up dramatically. "Hell, you sound jealous of Lotty."

"Jealous!" Jan sputtered. Jealous of a woman who had it all? Well, not talent, but certainly Charlotte Penn had the comfort of money, a gorgeous wardrobe, and a perfect complexion.

"Sleep on the idea, Jannie," Jason recommended and stomped silently out the door.

Jan was still staring after him, stupefied, when Doug leaned over and kissed her.

His lips barely brushed hers, but the feeling was so tender, she swayed toward him. "What was that for?" she asked when he sat back.

"For agreeing with me about the wraparound copy," he said quietly, then pushed back his chair. "I've got to go. I'm the chauffeur. See you in the morning?"

Jan nodded. "Early?"

Doug was already at the backdoor. "Very early," he said. He pushed the screen open, then closed it again. "For what it's worth, you're right, Jan. Having the Penns buy L'Amour would be a disaster for you freelancers."

"Convince Jase," she urged.

"As soon talk to the breeze, sugar. He won't hear a word either of us say. His mind is made up."

"Damn," Jan muttered as the door swung shut behind Doug.

Much to Jan's chagrin, when Doug arrived the next morning, the topic continued to be Jason's brainstorm.

Not that she expected him to be romantic at seven in the morning. But she had hoped for something a little more personal by way of a greeting than having a box of assorted donuts thrust into her hands.

"He's becoming a fanatic," Doug said settling

at her kitchen table with a steaming mug of coffee. He helped himself to a jelly donut. "But that's Jase all over, you know. He never does things moderately."

Jan peeked in the bakery box and selected a chocolate cake with nuts. "Did he hold you as a captive audience last night?"

"Nearly. He got on the phone with Clifford and Angie and I stuck around to find out what way the wind was blowing with them."

"Don't tell me," Jan said. "They were all for it."

Doug was noncommittally silent, concentrating on his breakfast.

"They were, weren't they?" Jan probed.

"I thought you didn't want me to tell you?" Doug grinned at her, his smile lazy with contentment.

"Oh, Lord," Jan moaned. "I know those two. Especially Clifford. He wants to write movies so bad he can taste it. Dangling that damn Penn woman's patronage before his eyes will have him on Jase's side. And Angie has always done precisely what Jase wants."

Doug took a second donut. "You know, Jan, if he pulls it off, you don't have to continue to work at L'Amour."

She sighed. "Oh, I know. But you've been in Richmond long enough to realize if I don't take assignments there, my chances of staying independent are mighty slim. There aren't that many jobs for freelancers." She studied the remaining half of her donut. Pressed her fingertip against pieces of the topping that had fallen on the table, then licked the chocolate off. "When this job ends, what are you going to do, Manhattan? Move on to Indy or north to Chicago? With your background, you should land an agency job easily."

"And spend my life playing with computer graphics?" he asked. "No thanks."

Jan's brows rose in surprise. Her eyes widened. "But you're good, Doug! I mean, really good. Any advertising firm worth a jot would kill to add you to its staff."

He didn't look flattered, only amused. "What about you, sugar? You've a rather deft hand yourself with a jar of rubber cement and a pair of scissors."

"Yeah," Jan agreed sarcastically. "I was a whiz in kindergarten."

Doug finished his second donut and leaned back, his long legs stretched out. "What would you like to be doing?"

"You're kidding, right?" she demanded. "I mean, look around you! This place is a factory, not a home."

"The same holds true with any artist's residence, Jan. Even in New York."

"Yeah, well, I'd still like to have a place devoted just to crafts." She stared into her coffee. "You sidestepped my question. Where will you go?"

"Depends," he said and absently took her hand

85

in his. He traced a path along her knuckles with his thumb.

Jan wished fleetingly that he'd said his future depended on her. Which was ridiculous. They barely knew each other. Still, it didn't hurt to dream.

"Depends on what?" she asked.

"On a number of things," Doug answered. "I'm investigating various investment routes."

"But graphics firms aren't among those various, I take it."

Doug had been concentrating on their linked hands. At her comment he glanced up with a wicked grin. "I'm probably the only one who doesn't covet L'Amour. Why not come with me on a tour tomorrow? It's Saturday. We deserve a day off."

Mentally Jan ran through the things yet to be completed on the brochures. There was very little to be done on the Penn Publishing project. "Okay," she agreed. "What kind of tour?"

Doug got to his feet and pulled her up out of her chair. "Historic homes."

Jan thought about what Doug had said for a good part of the morning. So when Jason breezed in the door with Charlotte Penn on his arm, it was only natural to expect to hear Jason announce that he'd convinced the Penns to buy Lloyd out.

There was no such news, however. Charlotte

simpered around Jason, pestered Doug with questions, and irritated Jan with suggestions. Cliff and Angie were an awestruck audience for Charlotte. It was all enough to drive Jan to drink.

At four o'clock she'd had enough.

"You hungry?" she asked Doug suddenly. "I've got the rest of Jason's chicken in the frig, and all those beers you left."

He looked temporarily trapped. "Sounds great, Jan, but . . . ah . . ." He glanced over to where Jason leaned against the back of Charlotte Penn's chair. "Well, I had other plans tonight."

She tired not to appear hurt. Every time she thought things were jelling romantically with Doug, something seemed to happen to cancel out that euphoria.

So what was new, huh? It had happened before. She should be immune to disappointment by now. Her romantic relationships with men didn't work out. She knew scads of men who considered her a good friend. One of the guys. She never seemed able to impress the kind of men who wanted to get married.

They were definitely of a specific type. Not one she had much of a chance of rubbing shoulders with. There had been many opportunities when she'd worked in the city. Businessmen were the marrying sort. Artists usually weren't.

They were too self-centered, for one thing, Jan mused. Too wrapped up in their creations to spare time for another human being.

Oh, they were amorous. It went with the temperament. Passion was everything. She'd felt that way herself once.

That was the trouble. She was caught between two poles. The girl her parents had raised wanted to find one special man to spend her life with. But the woman she'd become longed to be something more than just the little woman at home.

Jan trudged upstairs to her room. A soft, hot breeze edged in through the open window. She switched on a fan to augment it. Perhaps a cooling bath might improve her spirits. After that she would eat the rest of Jason's chicken and paint the elves she'd baked the night before.

She'd just started the bathwater when the phone rang. Jan's spirits lifted. It probably was just Jason calling to convince her his idea of luring the Penns to buy L'Amour was a brilliant move. Even arguing with him was better than brooding all night.

"Jannie?" It was her mother's voice. "I've got some good news and some bad news, sweetheart."

Jan sank back on her bed, the pillows plumped up behind her head. "Good first, Mom," she pleaded. "It's been a hell of a day."

"Simon remembered us in his will."

"Hey! That's great. Must have surprised Dad. He couldn't stand Uncle Simon."

"Your father is a stubborn man," her mother said, sounding pleased with the admission. "But so was Simon. It's a trait they shared."

"Yeah, well, at least Dad isn't obnoxious about it."

Her mother laughed. "That's not the way your Aunt Bea sees things. Which brings me to the bad news, dear," she said reluctantly. "Bea mentioned that she plans to visit you in Richmond soon."

Jan groaned and closed her eyes. "And I thought things were bad enough already."

Chapter Six

Doug sat slumped in an overstuffed armchair, his legs stretched out into the middle of the room. Across from him on the ancient sofa Jason regaled Charlotte Penn with a catalog of the paintings that had filled his life since leaving college.

The couple were in perfect harmony, each stroking the other's ego. Charlotte had never seen such life, such vigor, such a glimpse of the soul as she saw in Jason's canvases. Jason had never known such a versatile writer, one who could depict the greed in mankind's heart and yet show the tender side of human nature.

Doug had never heard such hogwash.

But, in an effort to waylay Jason before he could offer L'Amour to the Penn coffers, Doug stayed on. He listened to their fulsome compliments, watched them inch closer together on the threadbare couch. Wished he'd kept his nose out of this whole business and eaten leftovers at Jan's instead. Then at least he, too, could have been snuggled on a couch with a soft-eyed companion.

Instead he was the third wheel at Holloway's home, the voice that kept turning the conversation back to Charlotte's life in Indianapolis when it seemed Jason was about to bring up the investment possibilities at Amour Graphics.

Doug's years in New York were a definite plus. He dropped names like a veteran hanger-on, dazzling Charlotte with places he'd been, people he'd met. Or if he hadn't met them, and neither had she, he lied and described cocktail parties he hadn't attended.

And still Charlotte turned back to Jason, her eyes starry, her expression soft and tender. Her voice was mellow when she said Holloway's name. She couldn't seem to remember Doug's own name. To her, he was Stark Savage whether he cared for the designation or not.

He'd hoped to use that to advantage, to head her off so that Jason never got a chance to talk money and L'Amour. With her long blond hair, Charlotte could easily have been playing out her own fantasies when she'd written about Aphrodite's adventures. But somewhere along the way, she'd lost interest in old Stark. Charlotte had eyes only for Jason. And that reprobate was giving her his best hangdog expression.

Doug was beginning to wonder if he would end up spending the entire night as a self-appointed watchdog. It was past midnight and still Jason and Charlotte found things to gush about. L'amour was definitely in the air, but it had little to do with Lloyd's graphic shop at the moment.

The whole evening was a wasted effort on his part, Doug admitted reluctantly. Just watching the way Jason handled Charlotte nearly guaranteed the sale. Jase had honed his techniques back in college. Flattery, soulful looks, and the ability to keep his hands to himself. Women had clambered to break through that worshipful reserve. They'd never even suspected Jason's whole demeanor was an act.

It had disgusted Doug at school. It made his skin crawl now.

Maybe that was merely because he'd given himself a front row seat this time.

Charlotte wiggled deeper in the time-battered cushions, her eyelids fluttering coquettishly. "Is there any more wine?" she purred at Jason.

"For you, beautiful lady? Always," Holloway said. He glanced over at Doug, one brow raised to suggest that his friend go find a fresh bottle.

Doug chose to misunderstand. "Yeah, I could do with a refill, too. Bring the jug back, Jase."

Holloway was careful not to let Charlotte see the irritation in his face when he got to his feet. Doug watched Jason amble from the room.

"You don't have to chaperon me, you know,"

Charlotte said quietly when Jason was out of earshot.

Doug tried to look surprised. "Didn't know I was."

"Come now—"

"Doug," he inserted before she could call him Stark again.

"Doug," Charlotte repeated, her voice dropping to a very patronizing tone. "You see quite well that I fit in here." She waved negligently at the room, her sweep taking in the worn furniture, the dust, the litter of painting supplies.

The fact that Charlotte thought she fit into the bohemian jumble proved that she lived in a fantasy world. With her neatly pleated white linen slacks, her silk blouse, and Italian shoes, she was as out of place as a matched set of china would have been next to the chipped Melmac in Jason's kitchen cupboard.

"I really think you should go home," Charlotte suggested bluntly and gave him a thin, smug smile. "Because, you see, I don't intend to."

Women, Doug snarled silently to himself the next morning. Not only had Charlotte Penn shown her teeth the night before, now Jan Ingraham was behaving strangely.

The smell of baking dough permeated the

cozy farmhouse. Toasty-looking little creatures covered every flat surface in the kitchen as they cooled.

The temperature outside was already rising toward ninety and Jan was making it even hotter inside by baking.

From the looks of things, she'd been up until the wee hours turning out one batch of Christmas ornaments after another. There were dark circles under her eyes and a white dusting of flour nearly to her elbows. A dab of flour clung to her damp forehead. Her short dark curls stirred in the breeze from the two window fans that spun at top speed.

"Listen," she said when he walked into the hectic scene. "I'm on a roll here. Maybe you'd better just go without me."

On a roll? Hell, Jan was burying herself in crafts even though she'd known he was coming to pick her up.

Doug had been looking forward to having her at his side as he examined the list of properties the realty office had supplied. After the debacle the night before, he wanted to put thoughts of Holloway's plans far from his mind. Since being expelled from Jason's after a final glass of wine, Doug had expected to get a call from Holloway that morning to regale him with crows of success. Certainly Jason had gotten around to mentioning that Amour Graphics was for sale last

94

night once he was finally alone with Charlotte. If not, he sure as hell had said those fatal words when he'd woken up next to her this morning.

Did Jan sense that Jason had the upper hand? Was that why she was throwing herself into production? Doug glanced around the room again. En masse production at that.

There were tiny worry lines knitting her forehead just between her prettily arched brows. Her blue eyes seemed troubled, then looked away from his quickly as if she feared he'd read something in her expression.

"It was very nice of you to ask me along," she said, turning back to her mixing bowl. She grabbed the wooden spoon and dragged it through the stiffening mixture. "But I really can't."

Doug took the bowl away from her. Pried the spoon from her fingers. He took her floury hands, draped them over his shoulders. "Hush," he said and kissed her softly.

"But—"

He pulled her closer. Kissed her a little more ardently.

"I need you with me today," he murmured when they parted. "I want you there. I wouldn't have asked you to come if I didn't."

She looked down at his chin rather than meet his eyes. "But when you . . ."

Doug tilted her chin so that she was forced to look back up at him. His hands cupped her face. His thumbs traced the circles beneath her eyes gently. "Jan, I was trying to head Jase off last night before he could proposition Charlotte Penn."

Understanding dawned in her eyes. They were gentle, glowing with a special light now. "You did?" she whispered in awe. "Oh, Doug, I—"

He kissed her again. This time his hands moved down her back, molding her body to his. She stretched, lifting herself up to fit naturally against him. Her soft curves against his hard muscle.

He hadn't meant to start the day like this, with her in his arms. But he had planned to end it like this. Preferably in her bed. The way the adrenaline was pumping through his system, the bed wasn't even necessary. The kitchen floor would do.

It felt so good to have her responding in his arms. So right. She was just the kind of woman he'd needed, and hadn't been able to find in New York City. Jan was uncomplicated, natural. Today he'd finally been able to see behind her reserve, had known she was hurt that he hadn't stayed for dinner.

He wanted to bury himself in her, to forget the hassles he'd endured with Tina. Lovely Tina who wanted something he couldn't give her. Who had had nothing to give him in return.

But, Jan . . .

Doug pulled up short. Damn, it was happening much too fast. If it was happening at all. Was he reading things into the situation simply because he wanted it so bad? Was she melting against him out of a shared desire or out of appreciation. She'd surprised him by her response to him the day they'd done the cover for *Passion's Last Stand*. And they'd only been acting that day.

This morning she had read him as easily as he had her, had realized that he'd gone to Jason's last night not for himself, but for her. He didn't give two hoots what happened to Amour Graphics. But Jan did. He'd wanted to be her champion. And this was how she showed her appreciation.

He was as breathless as she when they parted. "If that was a thank you," Doug said, "it's not merited. I have no idea if Jason suggested Penn buy L'Amour. They kicked me out around one this morning. Charlotte had her own proposition ideas last night."

"So we don't know."

Doug kept his arms around her waist, enjoying the moment. "We know Jase. He'll do whatever it takes to get what he wants."

Jan sighed and snuggled contentedly within

97

the circle of Doug's arms. "I never knew he was so mercenary."

Doug chuckled. "He always has been. With other people's money."

"Ah, well, that's why I don't know that side of him," she said brightly. "I've always been as broke as he is."

Behind them the timer buzzed. Jan reluctantly eased from Doug's embrace. She donned oven mitts and slid another batch of ornaments out of the heat. Then she turned back to the stove and turned it off.

"Do you still want me to come along today?" she asked lightly.

Doug could hear the insecurity underlying her tone. She still didn't understand that he was no longer just passing through, that he intended to stay.

"Absolutely," he declared.

Jan pulled her mitts off. "All right, I'll come. Make yourself useful while I change, will you? Cover the dough with cellophane and stick it in the refrigerator. I won't be a minute."

As she skipped out of the kitchen and up the stairs, Doug leaned against the counter and breathed in deeply, savoring the scents of cooking dough, summer heat, and the lingering trace of her violet cologne.

It was happening pretty fast, he mused. But it just might be happening right this time.

* * *

When Doug mentioned historic homes, Jan had immediately conjured up a decorator's showcase. She'd attended one a few years before, held in a grand old Richmond house. A few of her own wreaths and dried flower arrangements had been used among the antiques and beautifully coordinated furnishings. A number of custom orders had resulted from her inclusion in the showcase.

When he pulled his silver-gray Isuzu Impulse to a stop in front of a weathered, deserted building on Route 40, Jan didn't understand immediately that they had reached the first stop on their agenda.

"Come on," Doug urged climbing out into the tall weeds at the roadside. "I don't have a key, but I didn't want a salesperson hanging on my heels the first time I checked things over."

Jan looked up at the two-story building. Constructed of red brick, the exterior had weathered to more of a deep pink shade. The windows were tall and narrow, a feature that promised ten-foot ceilings inside. There were two separate outer doors on the lower level, and strangely enough, one on the second floor. Once they'd all been a crisp white but the paint was peeling badly on all three.

Doug circled the structure, his eyes moving

from the missing tiles on the roof to the clogged eaves to the abandoned bird nest that nestled next to one of the chimneys.

Jan got out of the car. The flowering tops of the weeds brushed against her jeans, coming up past her knees. The undergrowth was so thick it covered her sneakers. The sunshine-colored goldenrod waved in the mid-morning light. Clumps of tiny daisylike dogwood were interspersed with wild wheat, purple and white clover, and a galaxy of other wild plants.

Thanking her lucky stars that she wasn't plagued with hay fever, Jan plowed through them, following Doug around the house.

He held out his hand to her, urging Jan to accompany him on his tour. "What do you think?"

"Well, it's not exactly what I was expecting," Jan admitted. "Doesn't look like much."

"Not now," Doug agreed. "But business was probably booming here in its heyday. The location was great."

Jan glanced back at the nearly empty road. The vehicles that traveled Route 40 usually had specific destinations just off it. Trucks and passenger cars traveling greater distances, or in more of a hurry, took the wider, faster way on Interstate 70.

"This was a great business location?" she echoed in disbelief.

"Was," Doug repeated with a bit more emphasis. "You know where we are, don't you?"

Other than west of Richmond, Jan had no idea what he meant.

"We're on the National Road, sugar. The first federally financed major road. It stretched from Cumberland, Virginia, to Vandalia, Illinois. There were plans to extend it farther, all the way to St. Louis, but they didn't materialize."

Doug's eyes glowed as he studied the building. Jan had a feeling that he would have been just as impressed with it if the whole place had been in ruins.

"This is a pretty old place," she said tentatively, still puzzled by his fascination.

"Not a good example of the late Federal style," he responded. "But I'd say it's still a bit shy of two hundred years. Maybe the title deed will say."

"Two hundred!" Jan looked at the place closer.

"Oh, it's had a few renovations over the years. The realty company says there's indoor plumbing now, and hot and cold running water. Electrical power was added sometime in the Forties. No central heating, though. Just the fireplaces."

Jan stared at the place. "What kind of business was it?" she asked, far from convinced.

"A coaching house probably," Doug answered. "The doors prove it was."

101

She was definitely confused now. "Doors?"

Doug smiled down into her upturned face. "You don't know anything about historic houses, do you? And you live in one."

"I took it because the rent was reasonable," Jan admitted. "If it helps restore your faith in me, I don't have central heating either."

Doug squeezed her hand and led the way around the building again. This time Jan took special note of various features. Like her own farmhouse, the tall windows were made up of small panes. The sashes rose on cords. She could see one was broken and dangling behind the glass.

She still didn't understand why multiple front doors convinced Doug that the place had been a coaching house. For that matter, she had no idea what a coaching house had been. When they reached the road again, she demanded an explanation.

"Simple, honey. It was the Quality Inn of its day. A combination restaurant, tavern, and motel. One of these lower doors was for the public and one was for the landlord's family. In those days people lived above their business, they didn't go off to work elsewhere, especially not out here in the wilds."

The countryside didn't look terribly wild now. There was little sign of the thick woodland that had covered the area. Farmers had cleared it long ago. Only small token woods separated the fields, acting like windbreaks. It was hard to picture the landscape appearing any different, although Jan knew in history class they'd told her what Indiana had been like before civilization. Two hundred years ago it had still been Indian country, hadn't it?

"I'm just taking a shot in the dark on the age. Could be as new as a hundred and fifty," Doug said. "Places over in Ohio will be older simply because the road went through there first."

Jan gave up wondering about the Indians. "What about the third door? The one on the second floor."

Doug grinned. "That was probably for when the snow got deep. Did you know that . . ."

Jan listened to one fascinating tidbit after another. They were fascinating only because Doug was so enthralled with his subject. The fact that he wanted to share it with her gave Jan a warm, pleasant feeling.

Doug knew quite a lot about the National Road, Jan discovered. He'd become fascinated with it while doing a paper for an American History class during his undergraduate years. It had been an interest that he'd shelved since then. Now he was indulging himself.

The act to build the road itself had been passed in 1806, he told her. It called for a right-of-way to be cleared through the frontier wilderness. A full sixty-six feet in width with a twenty-foot-wide road running down the center. When the surveyors had come through driving stakes for the workmen to follow, property values along the route had skyrocketed.

The road was progress, the vanguard of the flood of emigration that would populate the nation. Officially it had been known as the Cumberland Road. Paved with a combination of rock, gravel, dirt, and sand, it had served as the turnpike, the expressway of earlier days. Stagecoach lines had raced its length. Conestoga wagons had traveled it. Work on the road had been in progress in Indiana in the 1820s, but by 1839 work was suspended when the crews reached Vandalia, Illinois, and the federal money ran out.

"How would you like to drive over to Zanesville one of these days?" Doug suggested. "Once the Penn covers are done. Take a holiday."

"Go to Ohio? What's in Zanesville?"

"The National Road museum. It's terrific, Jan. I stopped there on my way from New York. They've got wagons and milestones, and . . ."

She let him enthuse on, amused to find he was a rabid historian beneath that rugged exterior.

"When we get back, I'll show you a book I

got when I was there. It's got a picture of this covered bridge over the Whitewater River."

"In Richmond?" she asked, dumbfounded. There had never been one that she knew about.

"Well, it was there a hundred years ago," Doug admitted. "Ready for the next place?"

They visited three different sites in all. The other two didn't have the distinctive set of doors to identify them as former coach houses. However, one of them did have a barn at the rear of the property.

"Now that's what you need," Doug said leading the way toward it. The foundation was set into a hillside so that the front boasted a stone foundation a full story tall before the barn proper rose above it. The wood was weathered to a dusty gray. Boards were missing, giving the place the look of a moldy chunk of Swiss cheese.

Jan surveyed it dubiously. "Because of the air conditioning?"

"Because of the space. Wouldn't take much to fix it up into a decent studio," Doug insisted. "A couple of cast-iron stoves for warmth. I'd put in a large picture window in the north wall so the light would pour in."

"A picture window in a barn? You sound like Jason. Does that mean you paint, too?"

He looked stunned. "Of course not. I sculpt. Once I find the perfect building, I intend to devote myself to art full-time."

"And starve?" Used to Jason's habits, Jan knew that no matter how brilliant an artist was, few could live off the earnings from their work. He didn't look like a man who would enjoy the hand-to-mouth existence that Jason thrived on. Like the one she enjoyed.

It took a moment before her sarcasm sank in. If he'd announced such a high-sounding intention to Tina, Doug thought, she would have been thrilled. She hadn't understood the reality involved in such a decision. That it had not been reasonable for him to pursue his sculpting as a career in Manhattan where expenses were high. Tina would have kept them high by insisting he hobnob with critics, attend all the gallery openings. She would have wanted a wardrobe to match each occasion.

"Starve?" Doug echoed. "I hope not. I'll have a sideline to support me." The blueprints for his own arts and crafts gallery were clear in his mind. But some aspects were still indistinct.

Jan waited for him to volunteer information. But Doug decided to clam up. He couldn't finalize his plans until he found the perfect property. Let his other venture be a surprise to her.

He took a last stroll around the barn with Jan trailing him, her expression still dubious. After returning to his car, Doug found she had disappeared. He retraced his steps and found

Jan on her hands and knees gathering what looked to him like tinder.

She glanced up when his shadow fell across her collection. Her eyes sparkled, the glints reminding Doug of sunlight dancing on the softly lapping waves of a blue lake. She hadn't looked this excited with his historic house tour. It took Mother Nature to give her that glow.

"Look! Grapevines!" she exclaimed. "Aren't they just perfect? Already dried, too. Look at these shapes!"

Doug hunkered down next to her. He picked up one of the branches. It curled and twisted back on itself. "Interesting," he allowed.

"Interesting!" Jan nearly crowed. "Doug, you don't know a treasure when you find one!"

He watched her scramble among the leaves and weeds for each delicate bit of wood. Her touch was reverent as she gathered them up.

Not know a treasure? He begged to differ. But his idea of one wasn't a scrap of twisted grapevine. It was a woman with soft dark curls and a childlike joy over the simple things in life.

"What makes these special?" he asked.

"The price. They're free and I didn't have to spend a day scouring the woods for them," she answered as she piled the branches in his arms. "You don't know how hard it is getting to find them. I've picked a couple of wooded areas bare in the last year. I was afraid I'd have to go searching for more complacent farmers with small, uncut forests I could raid. At least now I can put that off until next year."

Doug stared down at the large bundle of tinder he held. Jan was already collecting yet another bunch in her own arms. "Couldn't you just buy the stuff? I know I've seen it in supply houses."

"Obviously you know nothing about costs and keeping them down," Jan said getting to her feet. "Probably comes from having to buy your clay. Jase never understood when I dragged him out to help me harvest either."

This time it was Doug who trailed Jan back to the car. "You're telling me you got Jason Holloway into the woods gathering vines?"

"And rocks and wildflowers."

"Wildflowers? Doesn't he have hay fever?"

"So he says," Jan admitted. "I made him take Allerest and he was fine. Can we put these in your trunk? If I'd known we'd be able to find such great materials I'd have brought along bags for collecting."

Juggling the grapevines in one arm, Doug fished in his pocket for his keys then popped open the trunk. Jan lay her treasures in the back as tenderly as a mother would place a newborn baby in its cradle.

"I scrounge up as much natural stuff as I can throughout the year," Jan continued. "It makes my outlay next to nothing. And the house has got plenty of space for drying. I've got one complete room upstairs with bouquets dangling from the rafters and shelves for storing. I have a good-sized garden out back where I raise mint, lavender, violets, roses, bridal veil and a few other things. Most of it goes into potpourri."

Doug whistled softly at the list. "You're a very versatile woman, Ms. Ingraham."

She threw him a saucy grin over her shoulder and climbed into the car. "The word is thrifty, MacLeod. Your Scottish ancestors would appreciate that idea."

Doug slid behind the wheel and started the car. "Next thing I know, you'll be inviting me over for homemade noodles."

Jan laughed. "Dream on. That's far too domestic for me. Besides, I specialize in bread. But noodles sound delicious. I know a restaurant, well more of a cafeteria really, where they serve the best homemade chicken and noodles."

The thought alone was enough to make his mouth water. "I'm game," Doug announced. "Show me which way to go."

Chapter Seven

It wasn't just the thick homemade noodles, or even the thicker slice of apple-pie, or the fresh cream in his coffee that made Doug feel replete when he turned his car back toward Jan's farmhouse later that evening. It was the pleasure he'd had in her company that day.

He'd enjoyed sharing his enthusiasm for the coach houses. Had enjoyed her own excitement over the grapevines.

During a leisurely dinner, Jan had told him more about her crafts, surprising him with the diversity of the things she created. Mentally he compared her to his former fiancée, and wondered what he'd ever found to love about Tina.

She had been one of the fixtures of his life in New York, the showpiece who looked good in the slinky, short, off-the-shoulder dresses he had favored. Tina had known everyone who was anyone in the art world. She had no interest in being an artist herself, just in being seen with artists.

They had met at a minor gallery. An evening of too much champagne and too little sense.

He'd taken her back to his co-op, jokingly insisting it was to show her his sculptures. She'd shocked him by studying them with a professional eye and declaring he showed promise of becoming a success.

Until Tina had urged him to concentrate more on his art and less on graphics, Doug had considered his weekend dabbling nothing more than a hobby. Once the idea was planted, though, he found himself dwelling more and more on the possibility of a future as a sculptor and gallery owner.

Common sense was something inbred in him. He was no Jason Holloway, either in talent or temperament. He liked creature comforts. So Doug had started investigating the reality, the opportunities that would be open to him. He'd attended every gallery opening, every museum showing. But he'd also traveled out of the city to view and evaluate the shows in the outlying areas. He found them as good as, and sometimes much better than, the highly touted city venues. For one thing, they lacked the presence and aura of the pseudo-knowledgeable patrons who tended to fawn over the big names with lots of press coverage at the larger galleries. There was nobody Doug hated more than the snobs who dropped artistic buzzwords with only the slightest idea of what they meant.

There was an air of sincerity, of honest understanding and pure enjoyment of art in the smaller places.

His type of clay sculptures were made for universal appeal, not just for a few elite collectors to admire. Contacts were the answer, and, with his dream in mind, Doug had made plenty of them in the last few months. The end result would be not only his own workshop, but his own gallery.

When he broached the idea to Tina, she'd been appalled that he couldn't see the same big picture as she did, that he hadn't set his sights on the wealthy collectors.

Well, looking back now, Doug admitted, he couldn't see Tina ever fitting in with the lifestyle he wanted. It hadn't been the one she wanted.

He couldn't say the same about Jan Ingraham.

She was unaware of his plans, so when she began telling him about her yearly booth at one of the malls in Indianapolis, he was pleasantly surprised. She told him about the fun of the holiday season, of the other people there selling their wares, of the camaraderie they shared.

"I've tried to get Jason to be one of the concessioners but he always misplaces the paperwork," Jan said as they lingered over their coffee. "If he actually participated in one out of every three shows I give him information about, he'd have sold half the paintings he hoards in that drafty old house," Jan insisted. "But you know Jase. If he didn't think of it himself, he can't be bothered."

"That's Jase all right," Doug agreed. "What type of things do your other friends do?"

"Wonderfully original pottery, intricate designs from feathers, hand-tooled furniture, textured weaving, delicate impressionist watercolors . . . well, you name it. But that doesn't really tell you what sort of talent is involved. The photographs would give you a better idea."

"Photographs?"

Jan smiled slowly. "Sure. We banded together and made small portfolios for each other. Now when someone is at an art or crafts show that the others don't participate in, they can often get the rest of us commissions. I made an extra two hundred dollars that way last year from sales I wouldn't have had otherwise."

"Any sculptors?" Doug asked, trying to sound casual.

"One. He specializes in exotic bird statues—very realistic."

Doug tried not to look too eager. His own statuettes were entwined confrontations between mythological creatures and humans. Each was based on legends or folktales from around the world. There would be no conflict of style if he could interest some of Jan's friends in displaying their work in his showroom.

"Could I see the samples?"

"Sure." Jan pushed her chair back and stood up. "But only if you promise to show me some of your work."

Doug tossed a tip on the table and guided Jan from the cozy, family-operated restaurant, his hand on her elbow. "That sounds suspiciously like *your place or mine*," he said as they walked the half block to his car.

She laughed. "It does, doesn't it. Well, which shall it be?"

He was almost afraid of how she'd respond to his answer. "Yours tonight. Mine tomorrow?" he offered. He was rushing things again. Despite his good intentions.

At the casual suggestion, Jan felt her heart flutter. A dangerous sign. It hadn't done that in a long time! "Sounds perfect," she answered.

Doug took both her hands in his. He smiled down into her upturned face. "Say that last part again."

"Which?" Jan's lips pouted slightly. "Perrr-fect?" she purred.

"Mmm," Doug murmured. His lips brushed hers lightly. "That was a much better dessert than the apple-pie."

Her eyes brimmed with amusement. "Not as fattening either."

"But addicting." He kissed her again, his mouth savoring hers a moment longer this time. "Very addicting."

114

"I could use a larger helping myself," Jan admitted softly.

This time he dropped a kiss on the tip of her nose and leaned over to open the car door.

Jan wished she'd suggested a restaurant closer to her house. As it was, Doug floored the gas pedal along the nearly deserted country roads. They made it back in record time.

But the fates were against them once more.

Jan spotted the black sedan parked at the end of her gravel driveway when they turned onto her street. She had recognized the woman, although not the man, on her porch before Doug coasted to a stop at the side of the house. The couple sat on the swing, its gentle motion stirring the evening air.

Although she hadn't seen her Aunt Beatrice in a long time, Jan knew her immediately. Perhaps it helped that she'd been warned. Then again, it was impossible to miss the resemblance between them. Bea had turned fifty on her last birthday. Jan hoped she looked as good as her aunt at that age.

They shared the same coloring, the dark hair and blue eyes. Both were tall and willowy. Jan's curls were a gift from her mother's side of the family, though. Bea's hair hung in an elegant curve, just brushing her jawline.

The last time Jan had seen that jaw it had been jutting with disgust at Uncle Simon's funeral. Bea had spent her life thus far as a spinster at the beck and call of her elderly bachelor uncle. She'd been his housekeeper, his nurse, his secretary. She'd hoped to be able to benefit her immediate family with such selfless devotion. Her brother and his daughter had never made the least move to help themselves, though, when it came to getting in Simon Ingraham's good graces. And thus into his bank account. The rest of the Ingraham clan had not been so blind to their chances. Bea tried to fend them off, tried to get Jan and her father to butter up Simon. It hadn't worked. "I don't want or need a handout," Bea's brother had insisted. "Let the rest of the family take Simon's abuse if they want. Just leave me out of it." Of course, Beatrice never had. If the rest of the relatives wanted a way into Simon's bank account, Bea was going to make sure her brother wasn't missed when the vault doors swung open.

Her aunt's jaw was relaxed now, Jan noticed. Beatrice was actually smiling softly, as if she were pleased to see her niece.

Jan couldn't work up an equal enthusiasm. "Aunt Bea," she croaked, climbing out of the car. She threw a helpless look back at Doug, hoping he understood she was mystified to have company waiting at home. "What are you doing here?"

Beatrice eased out of the swing. She wore

116

black, her tailored suit and pearls looking out of place on the pleasant summer evening. Especially on her porch, Jan thought.

"Walter and I were in the area," Beatrice said smoothly. She gave Jan a cool hug, brushed her cheek against Jan's, and stepped back.

So much for a warm welcome.

"I'm not sure you ever met Walter," Bea continued. "He was your great-uncle's lawyer."

The middle-aged man came forward, hand outstretched. He gave Jan a beaming smile. "Your aunt and I have been friends for a good number of years," he revealed.

Quickly Jan introduced Doug and invited everyone inside. When they were settled in the living room with freshly made mugs of coffee, Jan was still puzzled over her aunt's visit.

Beatrice and Walter sat at opposite ends of the sofa. While Jan had been busy in the kitchen, Doug had emptied two of the dining room chairs and dragged them over to augment the seating. Perched on one of them, her steaming mug balanced on her knee, Jan searched for some topic of conversation.

"I didn't get to tell you at the funeral how sorry I was that Uncle Simon died," she lied solemnly. Funeral parlors made Jan uneasy. She'd put in a brief appearance before her nerve gave out and then she'd fled back to Richmond. But Bea would consider it bad manners if she didn't

117

mention the bereavement. And the whole thing would get back to her parents. It didn't matter how many birthdays you passed, Jan knew from experience. If your parents disapproved of something you did, they made you feel about five years old and grounded from watching your favorite TV program.

"It was time," Beatrice said smoothly. "The rest of the family gathered for the reading of the will. We missed you, Janelle."

Since it had taken place more than a week ago and she'd seen no reason to go, Jan knew she shouldn't feel guilty. But Beatrice's look said she wouldn't accept logical reasons for her niece's absence.

"It looks extremely bad considering the bequests were announced," Beatrice continued. "That can't be helped, I suppose."

She looked at the lawyer, Walter, as if cueing him.

The older man actually chuckled. "I don't think Simon would have minded. What do you remember about him, Janelle?" Walter's eyes twinkled. Jan doubted he was as somber over Simon's death as her aunt appeared to be. "Be honest now," Walter urged.

Jan glanced over at Doug and rolled her eyes. She hoped Beatrice hadn't seen her.

"Honest?" she parroted. "I didn't like him."

Beatrice's expression hardened.

"But then I didn't know him either," Jan hastened to add. "I played Scrabble with him once. He cheated something awful."

Walter's face was creased with smile lines. "Believe me, I know. You beat him at his own game."

Jan was really beginning to feel uncomfortable now. "Well, yes, I suppose so. I cheated, too."

Walter laughed. "Simon never forgot that day. Or you, Janelle."

Good Lord! What had Simon Ingraham done? Put a curse on her? Extremely possible. Aunt Bea had arrived on her doorstep, after all. That was certainly akin to a curse if Jan believed her father.

Beatrice was explaining to Doug how Jan had created a word to beat Simon. "I have no idea what it was, or what it was supposed to mean—Simon always came up with meanings for his nonsensical words. But I do know it was worth an unbelievable number of points."

"Ninety-three," Jan mumbled.

When Doug looked amused that she remembered the exact total, Jan was even more embarrassed.

"Hey," she said, "I thought it was worthy of the *Guinness Book of World Records*. If it had been a real word, it would have been."

"Remind me not to play Scrabble with you," Doug commented. He turned to the older couple. "Sounds like Ingraham was quite a character."

"To put it mildly," Beatrice said flatly.

Jan gathered her wits. "So, what are you going to do now, Aunt Bea? Since you took care of Uncle Simon all those years, I suppose he left you his money. You could travel, or . . ."

Beatrice's brows rose. "And what makes you think Simon would leave me his fortune?" she demanded, her voice haughty.

It was worse that Jan had ever thought a visit from her aunt could be. "Ah . . . because you looked after him?" she essayed.

"I received a salary," Beatrice informed her testily.

Walter reached over and patted Beatrice's hand. "Don't put yourself down, my dear," he urged. "Simon remembered you very handsomely in his will."

Jan was absolutely speechless when her stiff aunt gave the lawyer a melting look of affection.

"Very true, Walter. He was quite generous. But I feel quite certain that you had a good deal to do with the sum."

Why, Aunt Bea, Jan mused. *You're human after all!*

"It will keep me quite comfortable in my declining years," Beatrice said.

Should finally get you a marriage proposal out of old Water, too, Jan thought.

120

"But we didn't come all this way to talk about my future, Janelle. We came about yours," Beatrice continued.

Startled, Jan jerked her mug, nearly spilling the cooling coffee. "Me?" Her spirits sank even further. It had to be bad news. After all, look who'd turned up to deliver it!

"Nearly all of the family knows the contents of Simon's final will," Walter explained.

"Vultures," Beatrice murmured. "They swept down on us before he was barely cold."

"Perhaps we'd best warn you, Janelle," the lawyer said. "They aren't happy."

About what? That she hadn't attended the reading of the will?

"Simon couldn't abide them, you know," Walter continued. "But he liked to keep them dancing attendance on him. It was only when he knew his time was drawing near that he made a new will."

"As usual, your father couldn't be bothered to come to the reading," Beatrice explained.

Walter gave her another fond smile before continuing. "Simon left both Beatrice and your father each an eighth of the estate."

Well, the news wasn't bad then, Jan thought. "So Mom said. Now Dad will be able to buy that new car he's wanted."

Walter looked even more than amused. "More than one. I would say. The total is nearly a quarter of a million dollars."

"Wow!" Jan breathed, stunned.

"A very nice nest egg," Walter agreed. "However, it doesn't compare to what Simon left you, my dear."

Uncle Simon had left her something? Jan was sure she knew what it was. "Don't tell me," she urged. "He left me the damn Scrabble board."

The lawyer's smile widened. "He did indeed, Janelle. As a remembrance. But he also left you the bulk of his estate. My dear, you are now an extremely wealthy young woman."

An hour later, Jan was still thunderstruck.

"I don't believe it," she whispered, perhaps for the hundredth time since Beatrice Ingraham and the lawyer had left.

Doug had no such trouble. Walter had been too thorough in his listing of the assets of Simon Ingraham's estate. There would be grumbling from the disappointed members of the family, he'd said, but the will was incontestable. If nothing else, Simon had known how to thwart his relatives. He had kept them dancing attendance on him over the years with empty half promises. But the only family he actually liked were the ones who stood up to him and refused to be his puppets.

He'd paid Beatrice a salary for her work. Although she'd tried to curry favor for her brother and his family, in particular, Bea had never asked anything for herself. So Simon had rewarded her with a bequest.

Jan's father had always laughed at his sister's efforts to get him in Simon's good graces. He'd gone head to head with the old man long ago when Simon had tried to interfere in his life. The older Ingraham had actually offered a bribe to have his nephew marry the girl of Simon's choice. Jan's father had refused, wed the woman he loved, become a moderately successful businessman, and had never spoken to his uncle again. For some perverse reason, his nephew's attitude had appealed to Simon. He'd left a small fortune to Jan's stubborn father, pointing out in the will that there were no strings attached to the money this time.

But it was Jan herself who had impressed Simon Ingraham. She had her father's backbone, but she had a bit of Simon's own brand of grit as well. He'd never forgotten the way she'd turned the tables on him, beating him with his own warped rules of play. As far as Simon was concerned, that had shown she was worthy to be his heir.

Walter had explained it all, detailing his own talks with Ingraham. Telling how the doctor had been in attendance to ensure that Simon's bequests would hold up in court, that his mind had been sound, even if his reasoning could be construed as a bit twisted. To anyone who had known Simon well, the explanations were crystal clear. He'd been a cantankerous old man, but he'd been very successful in business. His ability to make money had been as sharp at his death as in his youth.

If Jan chose, she would never have to work again. The money could be invested to ensure a steady, healthy income over the years.

But Doug knew that Simon Ingraham had erred badly in believing Jan had inherited his grit. She might have turned the tables neatly on him the one time they'd been together. She wasn't the woman to manage a fortune. Or even to put it to good use. At least not the way Ingraham probably would have seen it. Jan had one quality old Simon had lacked—a very soft heart. It was part of what he liked about her. But, at the same time, Doug knew of one sob story that already had Jan's whole attention—mainly because she'd help create it.

Doug sat next to Jan on the sofa waiting for the moment when she made the fatal decision. For make it, she would. And once she did, the woman who had been ecstatic while gathering dead vines would be lost to him.

"This is an incredible day, isn't it?" Jan asked, her voice still dazed.

He had planned for it to be incredible, Doug

124

thought wryly. Only in a different way. Somehow making love to her now would be anticlimactic. Just a way of celebrating her good fortune.

The whole idea gave Doug a bad taste in his mouth.

"Amazing might be a better word," he said.

"Yeah," she agreed. "Who would have believed it." She gazed blankly at the Scrabble board Walter had left her. He'd waited to give it to her. As if it was the final token, the material evidence that she had actually become an heiress.

"You know what this means, don't you?" Jan demanded, her eyes beginning to sparkle.

Doug recognized disaster in the making. "Guys will be lined up at your door ready to propose marriage," he said dryly. "Charities will rush to tell you their heart-rending stories."

"No, silly." She smiled brightly at him. "It means I can buy L'Amour!"

Damn. She'd said it.

"Bad idea." Pointing that out didn't make him feel any better. She'd never see his view. Amour Graphics had been in her blood for weeks now. The hopeless cause that she'd dreamed of righting. Just as Jason had. Which was part of the problem. Ownership of L'Amour had now become a contest between the two old friends.

"A bad idea?" Jan scooted around in her seat to face Doug. "Are you nuts? It's perfect! We won't have the Penns breathing down our necks

125

now. We'll all have just what we wanted! Jason can use one corner for a studio, Cliff can have a place to write, and I'll have work and storage room. Since Lloyd and Sandy will be gone, Angie can run the front office. She can answer the phone and key in copy at the same time. And keep up with her afternoon soaps on the tube, too."

In all her planning, she'd forgotten one thing. "And who's to run the business? Who will do Lloyd's job? Someone has to be out in the community drumming up assignments, Jan. Who'll do that?"

She laughed, her voice trilling with undiminished excitement. "You're still thinking in Manhattan terms, Doug. The business is built in. That's the charm of it all. As long as we continue to undercut everyone else's prices, the jobs will pour in."

"Sweetheart, you need to step back from this. Look it over thoroughly before you jump."

Her face softened, but her eyes still glowed with that unnatural light. "Say that again," she urged sliding closer to him.

"You don't leap into investments based purely on emotions, Jan," Doug insisted.

Her arms went around his neck. "No," she purred. "You're not playing the game."

Oh, he knew the game all right. It was time for the celebration kisses, and all that should have followed. The things he'd been thinking about and waiting for patiently all day.

"Promise me you won't buy L'Amour," Doug said.

"Don't be silly," Jan whispered huskily. Her eyes dipped to his mouth, as if he actually needed a further hint of how to end the evening.

Doug dragged her arms from around his shoulders. His grip on her wrists was tight enough to hurt. "Jan. I'm serious. Leave L' Amour alone. Let the Penns have it. You don't have to do graphics work anymore. You don't even have to do your crafts if you don't want to. You're a wealthy woman now."

She didn't try to pull away. She stared at the hands gripping her wrists. Doug released her.

"This changes things between us?" Jan's voice was still soft, but it had lost the seductive purr. She sounded hurt.

"Oh, God," Doug groaned. He buried his hands in her hair, cupping her face. Her skin was like velvet, her hair like silk. Her lips were so tempting. And that insecure look in her beautiful blue eyes was enough to unnerve the most stalwart of men.

"I don't care about the money, sweetheart. But L'Amour . . ."

She pulled away from him, her cheeks flaring with anger. "You don't understand, do you?" She stormed to the other side of the room, as if put-

ting space between them was the only thing that
would hold her temper back.

"Jan . . ."

"How could you?" Her voice was bitter.
"You're new to this hand-to-mouth existence.
You still think like you were in New York. Well,
this is a different world, Doug. This isn't just a
small town, it's a community. And I'm part of an
even smaller community within it.

"I'm an artisan, and we look out for our own.
We have to. No one else is going to do it. They
see us as outcasts. Throwbacks to a different
time. We don't hold down nine-to-five jobs. We
don't have days off, vacations, or benefits. We
get by on our own, shaping our lives differently
because we want something that is alien to the
so-called normal world. We want freedom."

Doug started up, to go to her. She was wrong
in thinking that he didn't understand. He understood all too well. But he saw the pitfalls in what
she intended to do. Wanted to protect her from
them.

As if he had a right to interfere.

Doug sat back down. He had no reason to tell
her what to do with her life, with her newfound
money. Perhaps if the windfall had come in another month, even next week, he would have
had a say. He hadn't been given the time. Was
still a bit confused himself about what he wanted
from her. He wanted her physically, but did he

128

want more than that?

Jan's back was to him as she faced the dining room table. The top was littered with the bits and pieces of her crafts. He doubted Jan saw them though. Her thoughts were turned inward.

"They're my family, Doug," she said. "Jason, Clifford, Angie. Without them I would have fallen apart. They were there when I was down and needed them. I owe them. Buying L'Amour is a way of paying them back."

He couldn't be quiet, not when she was making the worst move of her life. "You don't owe them a thing. Hell, weren't you there with Cliff during his divorce? I know you snipe at him, but you're going out of your way for him now.

"And Jason. God love us, Jason." Doug took a deep breath. "Believe me, Jan, you've given Jase a lot more than he's given in return. I know the man, remember? Probably a lot better than you do. He's a parasite who'll . . ."

Jan spun around. Her eyes snapped. "Don't you dare. Jason is my friend. My best friend. He's been there when I needed him. He's pulled me in on graphics jobs, helped with the crafts. Been a friend."

Doug was on his feet now. It took two long angry strides to reach her.

"And he's safe, isn't he?" he demanded sarcastically. "The sainted Jason Holloway. The man who looks and never touches. The man who offers a shoulder to cry on but never tries to get you in bed."

Doug towered over her, but Jan was too mad to feel threatened.

"Jason is a *friend*," Jan said. "Friends don't overstep the bounds. Don't—"

"Don't make you weak, is that it?" Doug growled.

Her shoulders squared. Her chin raised in a challenge.

Doug took up the gauntlet. He pulled her against his body roughly. "I do make you weak, don't I, Jan?" he said, his voice still a deep, deceptive rumble, like the warning growl of a cornered panther.

She was trembling. With fury, Jan told herself. It had nothing to do with the feel of his hard body and the things his touch engendered. He was going to kiss her. She could read the intention in his face. And it wouldn't be like the tender kisses he'd given her earlier that day, or the dizzying one the day they'd posed for Jason. No, this one was to punish her, to show her her place.

There was nothing she could do about either. Jan felt as mesmerized as if he'd been a cobra and she just a tasty snack.

Her throat arched back, Jan stared up at Doug.

He gazed down into her eyes. So blue, so

wide. And, damn it, so trusting!

"The hell with it," he grated, releasing her. "Think about what you're doing, Jan. Think about it real good."

The sound of his car had barely died away when Jan picked up the phone and called Lloyd Amour.

Chapter Eight

He knew she'd done it the moment he pulled into the lot next to Amour Graphics on Monday morning.

It didn't help to admit he'd known Jan would make the call no matter what anyone said. Doug still felt disappointed that she hadn't taken his advice. It proved that no matter how far their relationship progressed, Jan still thought of him as the creep from New York.

Well, she didn't have to worry about him stealing a job from her. To keep his mind occupied after leaving her, Doug had studied the list of properties along the National Road and driven off to explore more of them. It hadn't kept his mind from Jan though. He couldn't look at a copse of trees without wondering if it sheltered a wealth of grapevines or other natural materials for her crafts.

He hadn't called her. Or Jason, for that matter. He hadn't wanted to be mixed up in their lives. After nearly thirty-five hours, Doug knew he couldn't escape being involved. They were his friends.

Although it was barely nine, Jan's decade-old AMC Spirit was already in the lot. As was Jason's weather-worn Chevy, Clifford's disreputable Honda bike, Angie's Rabbit, and Lloyd Amour's company van. In the couple of weeks he'd been part of the crew, Doug had never seen the group gathered this early in the day.

No one was working though. When Doug stepped in the door, he found himself in the middle of a party. A strangely bedraggled one at that.

Jan might have inherited a fortune, but it would be weeks until the will was probated and the money in her hands. The freelancers couldn't wait to celebrate her, and their, good fortune. With everyone bringing something, the service counter in the front of the shop was nearly groaning with food. They must have all cleaned out their pantries to provide the incredibly strange breakfast buffet. There were donuts, an assortment of bagels and cream cheeses, breakfast sandwiches from a fast-food restaurant, open cans of fruit cocktail, peaches, pineapple, and pears, a plate of crisp, cold bacon, small boxes of cereal, and a plastic bag of brightly wrapped bubblegum. The coffee pot had been dragged from the back. The smell of fresh-brewed decaf filled the air. Large cartons of orange juice and milk stood there invitingly, but they were ignored. It was the champagne that Charlotte Penn passed around that was the hit of the morning.

Charlotte was the first to notice him in the doorway. "Doug!" she cried, surprising him. It was the first time she'd called him by name without being reminded of it. Charlotte sailed across the room and thrust a plastic wine glass in his hand. "You're about five toasts behind. Do catch up."

He watched her float back to Jason's side, the full skirt of her dress drifting behind her like a train. Jason dropped his arm around her shoulders. Charlotte planted a light kiss on his lips and sipped more champagne.

On Jason's other side, Jan didn't even look at Doug. She seemed overly intent on spreading cream cheese on her bagel.

"Where did we leave off?" Clifford demanded.

Doug knew where the copywriter should have left off—about the first glass of bubbly. The man's eyes were already glazed.

"Lloyd was telling us what he and Sandy are going to do now that they can retire," Angie reminded them. Her blond hair was dragged back in a ponytail. Her expression was pert and glowing. When combined with her Spandex cycling shorts and oversized jersey, Angie looked about sixteen rather than twenty-five.

Glad that the attention wasn't centered on him, Doug eased off to the side and helped himself to a rasher of bacon.

While Amour talked about motor homes and retirement communities in Arizona, Doug tried to prepare himself for the coming confrontation with Jan.

She probably thought he was a jerk. He'd certainly acted like an ass the other night. Like a jealous ass.

It wasn't Jan who sought him out. It was Jason.

"Not celebrating?" Holloway asked waving his own nearly empty glass toward Doug's untouched one.

"Too early in the day for me," Doug said. No one here knew he'd never missed an opportunity to attend a champagne breakfast in New York.

Jason stabbed a peach slice from the can with a toothpick. "I understand you were against Jan's buying the place."

Doug found the stack of unused cups and poured himself some orange juice. "If you recall, I thought you were all nuts to want the place. I still think you are." He crunched another rasher. "How are you taking it? Not upset that Jan whisked it from under Charlotte's nose?"

"Why should I be?" Jason grinned. "It's all in the family yet. I get what I wanted either way."

"That's what I thought," Doug said. "So what becomes of Charlotte now? She still seems rather . . . taken . . . with you."

Jason's smile widened. "Yes, she does, doesn't

she. Curiously refreshing woman. Lotty has plans for me. Great plans."

"I got that impression when she kicked me out the other night."

Charlotte had Clifford in a corner now, talking excitedly, her hands waving. The champagne in her glass sloshed over the side.

"Is she going to become another name in the long chain of women in your past?" Doug asked.

"You mean, loved and left?" Jason chuckled. "Oh, I don't think so. Lotty's got two ex-husbands behind her. She's the one who does the leaving. And, in this case, I know on which side my bread is buttered."

Doug thought it would have been more apt if his friend had used the analogy of knowing a silk-sheeted bed when he fell into one.

"If you weren't already in the picture, I'd consider putting the move on Jannie," Jason said. "Wealthy women make wonderful patrons of the arts."

Doug tossed off the orange juice and wished he hadn't declined the champagne. Or that there was vodka in the orange juice. "Somehow I'm not surprised you'd feel that way," he said. It was amazing that his voice was calm. Inside, Doug was seething at his former roommate's cavalier attitude.

"It's great for us," Jason continued, unaware of Doug's tightly controlled anger. "I'll sponge off Lotty. You can shack up with Jan. Either way, we can both follow our muse while they foot the bills."

Jason had been callous in his treatment of women when they'd been at school. Back then, Doug had thought that it was a phase, that with maturity Jase would change. Instead, he'd gotten worse.

Well, Charlotte Penn could fend for herself. She was probably used to men like Jason, men who loved her for her money. At least he could run interference for Jan Ingraham, Doug decided. Jan was so blind to Jason's true character, the damn parasite would suck her dry, both emotionally and financially, if he got his filthy mitts on her.

"Looks like it was my lucky day when I decided to come to Richmond," Doug mused. "I'd best mend my fences, hmmm?" He picked up the glass of champagne Charlotte had thrust upon him. "By the way, how are you coming with those last two covers? Not putting them off to keep Charlotte kicking her heels here, are you?"

Jason stabbed another peach. "It's a thought."

Doug bit back a curse.

"But since Lotty suggested we pop down to the Bahamas once the project is finished, I'll have them done by midweek. Why? You thinking of getting Jannie to pose with you as Stark Savage again?"

And sink to your level? Doug snarled mentally. How had he ever stayed friends with Jason for so long? Was it only because Jan was involved that he was seeing what a sleaze Holloway really was?

"Not on your life," Doug said. "From now on, my posing is all in private. But the sooner we can get away from that damn layout table, the better."

It was easy to see that no work would be done that day. Doug waited until Jan was alone to corner her.

"I think I owe you an apology," he said quietly.

Her eyes flew to his, wide and glowing with relief. "No you don't. I was a bit emotional myself."

Doug felt as phony as Jason Holloway but he played his part anyway. The humble would-be lover.

She had a stubborn streak that got wider when she met resistance. She wouldn't listen to any advice, good or bad. All he could do was hang in there and hope she didn't get hurt. Jan had to discover for herself what he already recognized — that L'Amour wasn't what she really wanted at all.

"I was out of line in preaching to you the other night," Doug said. "It's your money. If you really want L'Amour that bad, I'm glad you got it," he said, hating every lying word.

"I did want it," Jan said. "Can we be friends?"

Doug wasn't sure if it was part of his performance or if he just couldn't resist the urge to touch her. He caressed the curve of her cheek with his knuckles. "If your aunt hadn't shown up, we'd be more than just friends already," he said.

Her cheeks flushed, her eyes softened.

Doug kicked himself mentally. She was falling for it.

"Maybe we could try again?" Jan suggested.

"I was hoping you'd say that," he said. "Shall we drink to the success of your new business?" He lifted his champagne. "I missed the earlier toasts, I'm afraid. We'll just have to have a private one."

Jan retrieved her glass from Lloyd's desk. "That will just make it more special."

They weren't private for long. Charlotte Penn pounced on Jan moments later.

"I'm so pleased for you," Charlotte cooed. "But I feel you are in need of guidance, dear Jan."

"Guidance?" Jan looked after Doug. He'd retreated to the hastily assembled buffet and was finishing off the plate of bacon.

Charlotte followed Jan's gaze. "No, no. Not with Stark, rather Doug, but in your new venture. You've never run a business before, have you?"

"Well, my crafts, of course, but . . ."

"That's what I thought," Charlotte said. "Guidance. You need to know how to go on. How to be a success."

"A success," Jan echoed.

"That's the whole reason one buys into an established business," Charlotte insisted. "Because there is the prospect of making a profit. You made an excellent choice with Amour Graphics. I had already done a bit of investigation with an eye to it myself before Jason told me it was for sale. You see," Charlotte said, her voice dropping to an intimate, almost secretive level, "the owner of a going concern like this doesn't always need to have retirement in mind to be open to overtures from a larger company. Penn Publishing was in the market for a graphics firm. We're still looking for a lithographer."

Jan breathed a sigh of relief. Uncle Simon's money had come at just the right time. Another week or so and the Penns would have snapped up L'Amour. Despite what Jason had thought, it sounded like Charlotte's father would have turned the small firm into a division of his publishing company. The chance to continue their own interests in the vast space of L'Amour would have been gone.

"Now the whole key," Charlotte continued, "is to look successful." Her eye skimmed over Jan's pastel blouse, worn jeans, and high-top sneakers. "Frankly, dear Jan, you are in need of major help in this category. But I think I can help you. Shall we say lunch today? I'll be back to pick you up around one."

Stunned by Charlotte's sudden interest in her welfare, Jan nodded blankly. Boy, she mused, when things happen, they happen fast!

Jan looked at herself in the mirror, a frown on her face. Even when she'd worked in Indianapolis, she'd never owned a suit. "I don't know. I don't think it's me."

"Nonsense. It's perfect. Wouldn't you say so?" Charlotte demanded of the hovering salesclerk.

Jan tried to forestall a *yes* response. "I prefer softer colors. Pastels. And flower prints."

"For business appointments flower designs are too frivolous. Pastels are too washed out," Charlotte insisted.

As if pearl gray wasn't, Jan thought staring at her reflection.

"It's so conservative," she said of the suit.

"It's supposed to be. You're a businesswoman now. You've got to look the part."

"I don't feel like a businesswoman," Jan grumbled. "And besides . . ."

Charlotte wasn't paying attention. She'd already turned to the clerk. "What else have you got? Something in navy blue?"

Jan felt her spirits sinking. Their lunch had been very brief, salads and the suggestion that they finish quickly to go shopping. It had been so long since Jan had even considered shopping without a specific item in mind, that she found the idea enthralling. Or she had until Charlotte took over.

"It's not that I don't appreciate your help, Charlotte," Jan tried. "But I can't afford to get these things right now."

"You can't afford not to," Charlotte insisted. "Besides, we're putting them on your charge card. By the time the bill comes in, so will your inheritance."

The clerk arrived back with another armload. Jan was depressed to see two navy suits in the batch. Fortunately there was also a gentle powder blue outfit among the offerings.

Charlotte tapped one manicured nail against her teeth in thought. "You'll need something for evenings."

Jan thought about her nightwear, a football jersey for summer and flannel nightgown for winter.

"A cocktail dress," Charlotte mused. "In red, perhaps."

"A what?" Jan choked. "Where will I wear something like that?"

Charlotte was never at a loss. "Why, at my party, dear. Didn't I tell you I found a house to purchase? The most perfect little place. Five bedrooms on two acres of wooded property just outside of town. Cathedral ceilings in the main

142

rooms. Jason's paintings will look wonderful. I plan to launch him, you know." She smiled smugly.

Jan watched the other woman's reflection in the mirror and was reminded of a cat lapping cream. She could almost see Charlotte washing her whiskers.

"Then I'm going to marry him," Charlotte announced. "Here, try this on." Charlotte handed Jan one of the navy suits.

Jan struggled out of the pearl gray jacket. "Marry Jason?" she said, as if she hadn't heard right.

"He's ripe for it," Charlotte said.

"*Our* Jason Holloway?" Jan was still sure she'd been mistaken.

Charlotte laughed. "Oh, he doesn't know it yet. Haven't you ever noticed the phenomenon, dear Jan? Men fight the idea of marriage, of course. But there comes a time when they weaken to the idea. The next woman along can coax them down the aisle with not much more than a crook of her finger."

Jan stepped out of the gray skirt and into the navy one. "It skipped my notice," she said. Well, what could she expect from the woman who'd dreamed up Aphrodite Cartwright?

"It doesn't work with all men," Charlotte explained. "For example, I have no idea of how susceptible your Doug is," she admitted. "It's the ones who aren't sure of themselves who tend to give off signals."

Jan buttoned up the jacket of the second suit. She still didn't like the way she looked, but the gleam in Charlotte's eyes said she'd just added another item to her bill.

"Then how can you know Jase's ready to take the plunge? I've never met anyone who is more sure of himself than Jason Holloway."

Charlotte's laughter rippled through the dressing area. "But it's all an act, darling! Just like that delightful beaten-dog look of his." She grinned more to herself in remembrance. "It's so endearing, don't you think?"

"Endearing?" It wasn't a word Jan would have used to describe Jason.

"You don't know him very well, do you," Charlotte said.

Jan had thought she knew Jason extremely well. She was no longer so sure.

"Well, not the way that I do," Charlotte added. "You haven't slept with him."

Jan had never even been tempted to. Jason was a friend. She'd never wanted him to be anything else.

The salesclerk arrived with a new offering. This time it was taffeta in a deep scarlet.

"Absolutely perfect," Charlotte cooed.

For once Jan had to agree. Even if she had nowhere to wear the gown, she knew she had to have it.

"You know," Charlotte mused, tapping her

144

tooth once again. "If Doug saw you in this, you just might find out if he's ready for marriage."

Jan's eyes flew to the other woman's. "Oh, but, I don't . . ."

"Of course you want to, dear Jan. Don't forget, I've seen you with him. That's wedding lust in your eyes, darling. Take it from a woman who's taken the trip a few times already."

Wedding lust. Jan cringed at the term. That's what came from hanging around with Charlotte Penn. She had nothing in common with the rich woman.

Well, that wasn't necessarily true anymore. After all, she was sort of rich herself now, Jan admitted. It took a while to get used to the idea. She'd been scrimping for so long.

But that's where the similarities ended. It was Charlotte who had wedding lust. The idea that it was directed at Jason still floored Jan. Jason?

Jan trudged up the steps to her room, the plastic coverings over the suits clinging a bit to her legs. She'd never been on such a whirlwind shopping spree in her life. It had been like compressing half a dozen Christmases into one.

They had exhausted Jan's credit line and moved on to Charlotte's. For a woman who'd lived in casual clothes for most of her life, she was still stunned at the idea that she now owned a dozen suits, assorted dress shoes, blouses, and a wickedly red cocktail dress.

Charlotte's campaign wasn't complete yet either. Tomorrow Jan was booked into a styling salon for a totally new look. And there had been mention of a car dealership. Jan's beige Spirit had been the first and only automobile she'd ever purchased, but Charlotte claimed that a successful woman wouldn't be seen dead in a vehicle more than a year old. Not only was the Spirit over ten years old, the company that had made it no longer existed. Charlotte had rolled expensive words off her tongue, BMW, Mercedes, and Rolls-Royce. Jan knew that Great-Uncle Simon was probably turning over in his grave. He'd never owned anything but a sedate Ford sedan. Black at that!

She hadn't been very successful at resisting Charlotte's suggestions while shopping that day. She'd have to strengthen her resolve, Jan decided. Perhaps it was time to replace the Spirit. Why not do it with something useful, like one of those sporty-looking vans?

Charlotte's expression of horror flashed into Jan's mind. No, she didn't think the idea of a van would go over well at all.

Charlotte wasn't the only person eager for her time, Jan discovered the next day. Lloyd Amour wanted to drag her around to visit the various accounts, to introduce her as the new owner. Jan put him off for a day. She wished she hadn't when the hairdresser began hacking at her curls that afternoon. With her hair moussed to a stiff cap, and her eyes highlighted with cosmetics, Jan not only didn't recognize herself, she hated the new reflection.

She managed to stave off changing cars that day by pleading a headache. Charlotte was very understanding, but adamant that Jan begin visiting dealerships soon.

Jan waved goodbye to her unwelcome bosom buddy, locked the door of her farmhouse against further intrusion, and stepped under the shower. With the mousse washed free, her curls bounded back, tighter now that they were shorter. Jan felt like crying. Instead she stayed up all night painting dough ornaments and thinking about how her life had changed now that she had money.

"Damn you, Uncle Simon," she said out loud. "You put this curse on me just because I won one lousy game of Scrabble?"

She could almost hear him laughing.

Wednesday dawned brighter, but Jan was far from in tune with the weather. She pulled on the pearl gray suit, and fastened a woven gold necklace around her throat. Real gold! Her thrifty nature rebelled at the thought. But Charlotte had insisted that the people she would now be dealing with would know the difference between costume jewelry and the real thing.

Successful women wore 18 karat, but Charlotte

lowered her standards to 14 karat since it was more readily available in JC Penny's jewelry department.

Jan shoved her feet into black pumps and raked a comb through her curls. Since there would be no avoiding Charlotte, she took time to apply mascara and put a touch of coverup on the circles beneath her eyes. Working late on craft items hadn't helped her get to sleep much before dawn. Ah, for the leisurely days when she made her own hours. But she'd promised Lloyd she would be ready to begin the rounds at eight. Jan couldn't ever remember breaking a promise to anyone.

Lloyd was on the phone when Jan reached the graphics office. "Five minutes," he mouthed at her. Jan nodded and strolled into the back. She was almost surprised to find that very little had changed.

The place tended to be deserted at this hour. Jason rarely was out of bed this early. Or Clifford, for that matter. Angie, always the follower, took her cue from them and usually strolled in around noon.

The lights were on over the graphics table though. Jan recognized Doug's tall form bent over it as he worked.

Guilt washed over her. He'd been hired to help her with the brochure layouts and now he was stuck doing them himself.

She stared at his back, thinking about Charlotte's comments. Was it really possible to tell if a man was ready for marriage? Or a woman, for that matter? Just because Charlotte said it was true, didn't necessarily make it so. Especially where she was concerned, Jan thought.

She wasn't thinking about weddings, but she was certainly feeling a rush of primitive lust.

As if suddenly conscious of her gaze, Doug straightened and turned. "Hi," he said.

"Hi." Jan felt self-conscious in her new clothes.

"You cut your hair," Doug said.

"Yeah," Jan admitted. "Charlotte's idea."

"Charlotte's full of ideas," he agreed. "Come here, I want to show you something."

Jan wasn't sure her legs would move. Was relieved when they did and she didn't wobble in the high-heeled shoes.

Doug had spread the completed layouts across the table. Only one was still in the final stages, the infamous *Passion's Final Frontier.*

But they didn't look like the same brochures Jan had labored over. The cover illustrations were no longer highlighted by frames. And the copy had been reset to wrap around them.

"You changed them!" she said accusingly. "After I told you that Penn Publications insisted . . ."

Doug held up a hand for silence. "I talked to Charlotte. Convinced her that you knew what was best for the sales materials. She gave the okay to fix things."

He'd talked to Charlotte! Without discussing it with her first? Sullen, Jan kept her eyes on the layouts rather than look at him. "It was your idea, Doug."

"You agreed with me. I distinctly remember the moment," he said, his voice light. "I believe I kissed you in appreciation."

Jan remembered that night. It seemed years ago rather than the week before. She wished she could turn back the clock to Saturday, then stop it before her aunt's arrival. Perhaps she could pick things up from that point. She could at least try.

"Does that mean I should return the favor now?" Jan asked, half afraid of what Doug's reaction would be. Other than the few moments they'd been together the other morning, she hadn't seen or talked to him since their argument.

Doug leaned back against the table, his arms folded. "I just might like that. But not here. Are you free later tonight?"

She'd make damn sure she was, Jan swore silently.

"I've still got your grapevines in my trunk," Doug said. "I'll drop them off."

Jan's spirits sank. He just wanted to clean out his car, not take up where they'd left off. "All right." Her eyes dropped back to the layouts. They really did look great now. His Manhattan touch. She doubted if they would have looked as good as if she'd done them. "You did a wonderful job," Jan said, motioning to the work on the table.

"Drop in the bucket. I wanted the new boss to look good. Secure Penn Publishing as a regular client for you."

Jan studied the layout of *Literary Liaisons*. Jason hadn't completed the cover when she'd last worked on things. It showed a couple grappling between dimly lit shelves of books. "You must have been working overtime to get these done."

"No sweat," Doug said.

"Still, I feel I should thank you. You've nearly finished the project."

He shrugged, his shoulders rolling with the smooth, natural motion that intrigued her. "Well, you could do one thing for me," Doug said, his voice dropping to a more intimate level. "Tell me what kind of wine goes best with grapevines?"

Chapter Nine

Jan shed the hated "success" clothes one by one as she trailed upstairs to her bedroom later that day. They made her feel like such a phony. But she had to admit, the suit had impressed Amour Graphic's customers. She'd met many of them over the years, but they hadn't connected the new Janelle Ingraham with the bohemian who'd done their work. Instead they were surprised that she was familiar with their past promotions. By the third office, Jan began letting them think she'd merely done her homework on the client list rather than try to explain that she'd actually created the items they considered success stories. From the way Lloyd's face beamed, Jan deduced that he approved of her new image. She knew Charlotte would have been proud of the way she conveniently left things unsaid.

The new Jan made the old Jan feel in desperate need of a shower.

Jan wished she'd been helping Doug with the mechanical pasteups instead of meeting her prospective business associates. She'd sustained herself throughout the day with pleasant anticipation of the evening to come. Her mind balked at actually dreaming up a scenario. She was too afraid that he'd just drop off her materials and leave.

Still, he'd asked about wine. That was encouraging.

With her suit discarded, Jan riffled through her bedroom closet. What should she wear? Should she be casual in jeans and T-shirt? Or should she try to look seductive?

For that matter, did she have it in her to look seductive? She'd never actually tried to seduce a man before. They'd never needed encouragement. Quite the reverse, in fact.

One item after another Jan considered and discarded. She even lingered over the red cocktail dress. But that would be overdoing it. She dug deeper and found just the right outfit.

She'd forgotten she had the sundress. It had been pushed to the back of the closet the summer before when the weather had turned cool early. At least she'd had the sense to put the dainty outfit in a garment bag. The scent of violets, one of her own sachet concoctions, enveloped Jan when she removed the dress.

Ah, this was much more like it, she decided, inhaling deeply. The scent was natural, not cloying like the perfumes Charlotte had tried to force on her during their shopping extravaganza. And the antique white tone of the eyelet fabric fit the woman she was, not the one she was being forced to become.

Pleased with her find, Jan filled her ancient clawfoot tub with tepid water and added violet-scented bath salts. With her dress airing in the breeze from the window fan, Jan cooled off, letting her body relax in the soothing bath.

Dusk was falling as she dressed. But when she surveyed herself in her mirror, she was far from satisfied. She looked sweet. And that wasn't exactly the image she wanted to portray.

It took only a moment to hunt up a pair of scissors, another to wiggle out of the dress and snip the wide shoulder straps away.

Dressed once more, Jan smiled at her reflection. Perfect. Absolutely perfect.

The dress had been fashioned to resemble an old-fashioned camisole and petticoat. The bodice buttoned up the front and fit snugly. If she was careful when she moved, Jan decided, it wouldn't fall down. The skirt swirled past her knees before flaring wider with the addition of a deep ruffle. A simple straw-colored belt of braided natural fiber wrapped around her waist before spilling down the front of the skirt. Jan slid into pale beige espadrilles and spent a good bit of time fussing with her newly shorn curls. No matter what she did with her hair, it looked tousled. After a nearly sleepless night, her eyelids drooped a bit, too. Jan hoped the combination made her look sexy.

She fervently hoped Doug would agree.

The fireflies were out in force that evening. Jan sat on the porch, letting the swing sway gently to and fro. After swatting at the mosquitoes that homed in on her bare shoulders, she gave up and went inside.

She'd already turned the radio to her favorite soft rock station. The mellow strains of an old Doobie Brothers' ballad etched into the night. Jan switched on one of the lamps near the sofa, keeping it on the lowest setting. The soft glow enhanced her skin, throwing shadows in the hollow of her throat and along her collarbone.

Jan glanced at her wristwatch. Doug hadn't mentioned when he would be coming by. It was nearly nine. Surely it would be soon.

She picked up a magazine, one of the batch her mother had dropped off during her last visit. She leafed through it, not seeing any of the features. When she finished it, she reached for another.

Nine-fifteen. Any minute he'd be pulling up before the house, would be striding across the lawn and onto the porch.

Doug stared at the glowing digital display of the clock on his dashboard. Ten-thirty. He hadn't meant to arrive this late. But Jason had finished the last of the paintings for the covers. After one glance, Charlotte hadn't wanted to waste any time. She'd faxed copies of the layouts to her father for approval then waited for him to call back. Both Penns were pleased that things were moving ahead of schedule, and as a result, pushed their publication date up. With Penn's final okay on the mock-ups, Doug had plunged into work on the mechanical pasteups, trying to finalize the sales fliers that afternoon.

And evening, he reminded himself with another glare at the clock. Fortunately, he'd already bought the wine.

He'd planned to be at Jan's around eight but, as usual, when the pressure of a deadline was on, he lost track of time. He hadn't realized how late it was until his back had started complaining about his slumped stance over the layout table.

Because Jan had already laid the groundwork on the mechanicals, the work had progressed at a good rate. They were almost ready to go to the lithographer.

Working on L'Amour's stuff hadn't been what he'd planned for the evening though.

Ten-thirty-two. She probably wouldn't even speak to him at this hour. He should have called. But that gave Jan a chance to hang up on him, to tell him to drop dead. And he wanted to see her. So, rather than take a chance with the phone, he'd jumped in his car.

Doug coasted to a stop before the farmhouse. A light glowed in the front room. Once he turned off the engine he could hear music playing.

If he was lucky, she'd gotten involved with her crafts and hadn't noticed the time either.

If not . . .

He took a deep breath, picked up the bottle of wine and climbed out of the car.

If she heard the door slam shut behind him, Jan didn't make a move to come to the screen. The house stayed as quiet and serene as it had been before.

Doug moved up to the porch, took the steps in a single stride.

And still there was no welcome.

His footsteps echoed on the wooden floor of the wide veranda. He reached the screen door, knocked lightly.

No answer.

He could see her now. Curled up on the sofa, one hand beneath her cheek, Jan was sound asleep.

The lamplight spilled over her disheveled curls, over a vast expanse of creamy white skin. Her long dark lashes lay lightly against

157

her cheek. Her breathing was soft, shallow, but it caused the lush upper curves of her breast to rise from, then fall back into, the low cut of her bodice.

Doug eased into the house, carefully closing the door behind him. He put the wine aside on the dining room table and moved over to the sofa.

Jan hadn't heard him. She slept on.

Like Sleeping Beauty.

Doug knelt on one knee next to her. He lifted her hand to his lips, kissed it then ran his tongue across her knuckles.

Jan sighed in her sleep and turned slightly.

Doug continued his exploration, tasting each of her long, graceful fingers. Unlike Tina's, Jan's nails were short and unadorned. The cuticles were pale half-moons, like the one that hung in the night sky outside.

She arched with pleasure and groaned slightly when his mouth moved up her arm planting light kisses on her cool skin. Her unconscious responses were heady to a man who moments earlier had been unsure of his welcome. Jan smelled of spring flowers and tasted of the sweetest nectar. Doug braced himself against the back of the sofa and the cushions, barely touching her. When his mouth reached her bare shoulders and cruised toward the sensitive hollow in her throat, Jan stirred, waking.

158

She dreamed that she was on a moonlit beach. Waves lapped softly around her, inched higher up on the sand then retreated. They touched her, fell away, and washed over her again, their touch gentle and erotic. Oh, so erotic. She stretched as a tingling sensation began at her fingertips and rushed through her body, building speed until it filled her being. It made breathing difficult so that she gasped at the cool night air.

It was no longer cool, though. It was hot and moist. The waves, she thought, and knew she was wrong. Waves didn't make you want to writhe with pleasure.

"Jan."

Her name was like a rush of wind. Warm, hot wind. It lingered on her skin, brushed against her cheek.

"Mmm?" she purred, sleepily.

"Jan," the voice said again.

This time she knew it was not the night air that called her. It was a man. A beautiful man with the deep voice of a panther, and the touch of an artist.

She moved languidly, sliding into his arms. Her mouth opened under his, welcoming the exotic caress of his tongue as it glided along hers.

Doug's fingers clenched in the soft upholstery of the couch. He held himself away from her, letting Jan rouse slowly. She was so lovely, so sweet and tempting in her sleep. The more she responded, the harder it was not to touch her.

Jan reclined back against the cushions, her teeth sliding across his bottom lip, tugging at it slightly. The bodice of her dress slipped lower over her breast. Doug's gaze dipped to the gentle rise, to the buttons that strained over her breastbone.

He took a deep breath and tried again. "Jan?"

Her lashes lifted slightly, dropped again, and opened. Her eyes were cloudy with sleep, and awakening passion. "Doug," she said.

It sounded like a sigh. Especially when she smiled softly, slid her arms around his neck, and pulled his head back down to hers. Her lips teased, taunted, and pleasured his. Jan's fingers slid into his hair, along the straining breadth of his shoulders.

His control snapped as easily as a worn piece of twine. With a low groan, Doug dug his hands into her soft curls, ground his mouth against hers.

She turned, arching toward him, into his arms, and tumbled off the sofa. Doug rolled with her, softening her fall with his body. Jan didn't seem to realize she now lay sprawled against him on the floor. Her hands were

160

against his chest, her breath mingled with his.

Doug ran his hands down her spine, touched bare shoulder blades, slim waist, and moved lower over her hips. Jan squirmed with pleasure.

"Mmm," she purred again. "What took you so long?"

Doug's mouth moved down her throat in a sensuous glide. Hot and damp and oh, so good.

"Mechanicals," he murmured against her collarbone.

"You're very good at these mechanics," Jan said in a sigh.

"I'm feeling inspired again," Doug whispered. "Very inspired."

Jan arched back from him. Doug's lips dropped lower, skimming along the rise of her breasts. His hand moved up along her ribs, to the buttons of her bodice. One by one he released them until her breasts spilled free. It wasn't his hand, but his lips that explored the newly exposed flesh. When his tongue found and circled one excited nipple, Jan moaned deep in her throat.

Doug rolled over, pinning her beneath him on the braided rug. "Not afraid I'm trying to dazzle you with my New York ways?"

Jan ran her hand down his chest toward his belt. "I could get to like your brand of expertise, Manhattan," she purred. "What else have you got to show me?"

Doug sucked in his breath as her fingers pressed lightly along the straining front of his jeans. "Quite a lot and very soon if you're not careful," he said.

Jan's laugh was low, husky, and definitely feminine. "Any fast moves?" she asked.

"Mmm, them's fightin' words, darlin'," Doug drawled. "Guess I'll just have to show you different. My great granddad was from the deep South," Doug murmured. "They like to move slow down that-a-way. And, when I put my mind to it, sweetheart, I can creep like a Georgia native." He nibbled lightly at the corner of her mouth then ran his lips down the arching length of her neck. Jan squirmed beneath him. "Before I'm done with you, sugar, you'll be begging me to act like one of those jackrabbit Yankees."

Doug nuzzled aside the fabric of her bodice. His hand slid over her abdomen, along her thigh, and found its way beneath her skirt. His touch was insistent, his skin rough against hers. He retraced his path, this time pausing at the junction of her legs.

Jan quivered in anticipation.

"Or we could go a different route," Doug suggested. "I could try one of ole Stark Savage's moves."

His lips returned to crush Jan's. She grasped at his shoulders, then gasped as Doug's fingers found their way inside her panties, and slid into her more intimate set of curls.

"Hard decision," she murmured a bit breathlessly.

"It isn't the decision that's hard, darlin'," Doug said. He leaned back, got to his feet and pulled Jan up. Slightly embarrassed, she tried to pull her bodice back together. Before she realized his intention, Doug's arm slipped around her waist, crushing her blushing flesh against his chest. "Don't," he whispered. "You're too beautiful to hide tonight."

Jan glanced nervously toward the open windows, toward the screen door. Toward the lights that gleamed from the adjacent housing development. "But the neighbors . . ."

"Let them be jealous," Doug said. "You know, there's a lot to be said for ole Stark."

"There is?"

"He's got a certain flash." Doug bent quickly and swept Jan up in his arms.

She felt like they were reenacting the moment when they'd stood bathed in the bright spotlights in the workroom at L'Amour. Her skirt spilled toward the floor. Her arms were linked around his neck. Only this time the look in Doug's gray eyes wasn't amusement. They swirled with emotion, were dark with passion.

Ah, sweet passion. She'd missed it.

"As romantic as it sounds, sugar, I think we'll forgo the rug burns tonight in favor of a nice soft bed," Doug whispered, striding toward the staircase. "You don't mind, do you?"

Jan let her head rest against his shoulder. "Not at all. In fact, I think it's absolutely perfect."

Doug squinted when the first ray of early morning light fell across his face. Eyes squeezed shut, he swore silently. Hell, why hadn't he remembered to close the damn blind last night? He opened one eye again, ready to grope for the cord and found the main reason he had forgotten was that there was no blind, only a token curtain of peach-colored chintz. Rather than block out dawn's damn early light, it framed the window, stirring gently in the breeze from a window fan.

He wasn't in his apartment. He was at Jan's farmhouse. In Jan's bed.

Doug leaned back against the pillow, content just at the thought.

He hadn't paid much attention to the decor the evening before. But now that he looked around, he found the place looked just as he'd pictured it. The bedstead was of the old iron variety, painted a simple white. Its springs had twanged a merry accompaniment to his love-making. If he stayed around, they definitely were going to get a good oiling.

Beside the bed stood an old-fashioned stand with long curved legs. On it reposed a delicately blown antique glass bowl filled with a fragrant potpourri of petals and leaves. Behind the bowl was a framed picture of a woman who resembled Jan, her dark hair in the popular Gibson Girl upsweep of her time. Her stiffly posed form, the sweeping length of her skirt, the matronly fit of her white blouse, and the sepia tint of the photograph clearly proclaimed the lovely subject one of Jan's ancestors. A twist of ribbon and lace held a peach-colored dried rose in a corner of the frame.

The arrangement was simple, but elegant. As was the rest of the room. The walls were papered in a pale pattern of tiny flowers. A single grapevine wreath hung opposite the bed, a scattering of wildflowers and more peach-colored roses entwined with the branches. In the corner was a full-length oval mirror on a stand. An antique clothespress and dresser rounded out the furnishings. Braided rag rugs picked up the hint of peach once more.

The room was homey, comfortable, utilitarian. It was the antithesis of Tina's New York apartment. There chrome, glass, and leather dominated. Even in the bedroom. To Doug it had always seemed so colorless and impersonal.

He glanced again at the fading portrait of the turn-of-the-century beauty. Ah, yes. He liked Jan's room much better.

At his side, Jan sighed in her sleep and snuggled deeper into her pillow. Her dark curls were tangled. A faint blush mantled her cheek. Above the sheet, her shoulders were ivory, bare, and artistically perfect.

A rush of affection swept Doug. It would take only a few lingering kisses to rouse her from her sleep. He knew from the evening before how pleasant the procedure was. Knew he wanted to repeat it often.

The thought jarred him more fully awake. Often? How often? Good God! The idea of making it a daily pleasure persisted in his mind. Daily? As in the rest of his life?

Something contracted in his chest at the thought — fear.

A lifetime! Hell, that wasn't what he wanted. Was it? He'd almost made a mistake with Tina. He'd barely shaken off the shackles of his previous engagement. He wasn't ready to commit himself to any one woman.

Jan sighed in her sleep.

Damn, but the idea appealed to him. If it were *this* woman.

He had nothing to offer Jan but an uncertain future. His plans were nebulous. They might succeed. They might fail miserably, leaving him with a mortgage on an isolated property set back on a forgotten highway.

Perhaps if her own future had continued to be ambiguous, he would have chanced asking her to share his dream. That opportunity had vanished with the appearance of Simon Ingraham's fortune. Jason might feel no remorse at making up to Charlotte for her money, but Doug was a different kind of man. The old Jan would have known how to juggle an uncertain future. He wasn't as sure about the new Jan.

Not just the money kept him distant, but also her muleheaded decision to buy Amour Graphics. She had rushed into it without taking into consideration that she was purchasing a business. She had seen it as securing a future income for her friends, as a place where she could do her crafts and they could pursue their own interests.

L'Amour was changing Jan's life. Would she adapt to the new responsibilities? Would she become the type of woman he'd known and worked with in New York? Her wardrobe already reflected that woman. The tailored suits, the shorter curls, the touch of mascara darkening her already dark lashes. Were the changes all just on the surface, or was Jan slowly becoming another Tina? A manipulator determined on her own success, no matter what it took, or whom she hurt?

His own brand of success hadn't been what Tina had wanted. He hadn't wanted it to be.

How would Jan Ingraham rate his chances of making a name for himself as a sculptor?

Did he even want to find out?

Doug eased out of the bed, dragged on his jeans and crept away. Until he knew what he wanted, his most sensible decision was to put space between them. Time would tell if what he felt was love or just garden variety lust.

Jan slept on.

Chapter Ten

Charlotte Penn was on hand when Jason's illustrations were screened for four-color separation. But the Penn Publication sales brochures went to press without Jan.

Lloyd was anxious to turn over the graphics company to her and head west to begin his longed-for retirement. Jan was forced to make use of her hated wardrobe of suits as Lloyd found new places to drag her each day. She learned to deal with the photographer, the lithographer, the telephone company, the tax department, the realty company, and, worst of all, the accountant. By the end of the week, her head was reeling with information.

But the worst was yet to come. Walter, the lawyer, called from Indianapolis insisting that she was needed in person to deal with various issues arising in the settlement of Simon Ingraham's estate. Her great-uncle had chosen to divide his fortune between just three relatives, but he had not issued instructions on which assets were to go to Beatrice, to Jan's father, to

Jan herself. The three of them were forced to spend the best part of a week with Walter sorting things out.

And in all that time, Jan didn't see or speak to Doug.

At first she wondered if she'd dreamed the evening in his arms. But the indent of his head on the pillow next to hers that morning, and a table full of grapevines downstairs, had reassured her.

She'd gotten up and dressed, her mind dwelling on rose-colored pictures of working next to him over the layout table at L'Amour.

Jan even conjured up another late-night use for the wide table.

But when she reached the graphics office she found that the mechanical pasteups were done and ready for the offset-lithographer. And that Doug had already bowed out of L'Amour.

Lloyd was full of praise for the former New Yorker's work, comparing it favorably, in a burst of diplomacy, to Jan's own skills. Without Doug's help and long hours they would never have met the new Penn deadline.

Jan winced at the reminder. It didn't matter that between Lloyd and Charlotte she'd been unavailable to do her old job. It still hurt to hear another graphics person praised over the work.

Lloyd was surprised to find neither Jan nor Jason had any idea of where Doug had gone. After finishing the brochures, the man from

Manhattan had disappeared. There was no answer at his apartment when Jan gathered her courage and called. There were no phone calls from Doug that night either.

Jan fretted. What had she done wrong? Had she been too eager?

Had her heart been too clearly displayed?

Distressed to be found wanting, and ignorant of her failings, Jan tried to bury her feelings in work.

There was more than enough to take her mind off her romantic failure. She was drowning in a sea of details at Amour Graphics.

Work didn't cure the depression, nor did it ease it. Jan swung like a pendulum between feeling that Doug had usurped her project and wondering if she'd really been unexciting in bed.

She waited three days before questioning Jason. But he had no idea what had happened to his friend. Nor did he care. His own life had somersaulted; he was too caught up in Charlotte's decision to launch his real art career to worry or wonder about Doug.

But in the evening, when she returned home, Jan found new strength. The light on her answering machine was blinking, brightly excited that it had a message to relay. Expecting it to be a call from her parents, her aunt, or the lawyer, Jan pushed the play button and dropped down on the sofa to listen.

Doug's voice startled her at first, then the

sound of his deep tones washed over her, soothing her. "Hi, beautiful," he murmured. The greeting, more of an endearment, was a definite, vocal caress. "Sorry I ran out on you the other morning," he said. "Believe me, I've been kicking myself ever since. I'm temporarily taking the search for properties further away from Richmond. See you when I get back."

Jan ran the message back, replayed the first two words, then switched the machine off.

She felt much better. For the first time in days, she was hopeful.

In the ensuing days her ego was stroked further when more of Doug's messages turned up on her machine. Jan began to wonder why he didn't call in the evening when she was home. Why did he always phone when he knew she was gone? But beggars couldn't be choosers. If recorded words were all she got, well, they were a damn sight better than no words at all.

Two messages were waiting when she got back from Indianapolis.

"Hi, sugar," Jan decided she preferred being called *beautiful*. "Still keeping a candle burning?" Doug's voice crooned. "Picked up some nice twigs for you today. If they aren't suitable for craft use, maybe we can toast marshmallows over them this winter."

Jan hugged herself at that casual hint of a future together. But the best message was the last and briefest one.

"Miss you," he said, his voice pitched low and a bit husky. There was a long pause then he added in a still more intimate tone, *"a lot."*

Jan sat and stared at the answering machine. "Me, too," she said wistfully.

The message should have raised her spirits to new heights. Instead, it sent them plunging. She wished Doug would get back to town soon. She needed someone to talk to, someone who cared about her. Because, at L'Amour, she was beginning to feel like an outsider.

There was no one she could confide in. Her friends had always been the people she worked with—and they made excuses to avoid her now. Feeling more and more confined, Jan continued to pull on a suit every morning and to bury herself in the day-to-day hassles of being a businesswoman.

The grapevines she and Doug had gathered stayed on the dining room table, soothing evidence that he had come to her that single night.

Lloyd turned over his appointments to her, disgustingly happy to be free of commitments. Jan wished he hadn't done so. She was very uncomfortable dealing with clients. Her expertise was with a pair of scissors, with decisions on type sizes and styles, with the actual creation of a logo or advertisement. Discussing prices and deadlines with people who had no concept of what was involved in the mock-ups or the variations in paper quality or impact of different colors of ink gave her a headache.

Jan returned to the graphics office late in the afternoon from one such appointment. The fact that L'Amour had been awarded the job didn't cheer her. She had been running from one business meeting to another ever since the night Beatrice and Walter had come to see her. She wanted a respite. Wanted a vacation. More importantly, she wanted to get back to her crafts.

Rather than take her newly acquired briefcase home with her, Jan swung by Amour Graphics to dump it on her desk. Since it was long past five, it jolted her to find the parking lot still full. With the Penn project at the printers, she hadn't expected to find any of her friends still there.

Perhaps they were just moving in, she thought. Jason's easel and paints hadn't made an appearance yet. Neither had Clifford's books and file cabinets. Fleetingly, Jan wondered when she'd get a chance to begin expanding her crafts business by moving materials to the back of the shop.

The office itself was deserted, but that had always been a natural state of affairs. Because Lloyd and Sandy were in and out so much, they had put a bell on the counter so that customers could summon one of the freelancers in the back. The system had worked well in the past. Jan hoped that it would in the future. That the time would come when she could sit in the workroom and do crafts rather than troop around town visiting clients.

Jan pushed through the swinging double doors into the back and found the workroom was unchanged. No effort had been made to turn the vast room into separate work areas. Instead her friends were clustered around the graphics table.

Brochures depicting travel trailers and retirement villages lay scattered on the surface. Lloyd was discussing the advantages of various cab features with Clifford. Jason and Angie were arguing the merits of Phoenix over Tucson for the Amours' more permanent home.

The scene amused Jan. They were all so opinionated. To hear Cliff talk, he was intimately acquainted with the most luxurious of motor homes. This from a man who rode a disreputable Honda motorbike and lived in an ancient, single wide trailer. Jason and Angie were no better. They each sounded like they had personally investigated places in Arizona with an eye to buying property. As if either of them had the funds or had ever been more than a hundred or so miles outside of Richmond.

Still, the whole setting was so reminiscent of other afternoons, Jan felt a rush of nostalgia.

And remorse.

She no longer belonged to the group. Not only was she out of place in her suit and heels, she had become the boss. The title set her apart.

Despite the fact that she now drove around in

the comfort of an air-conditioned car, one of the many features on the Oldsmobile she and Charlotte had compromised over, Jan was uncomfortable.

Angie looked much more at ease in her walking shorts, T-top, and sandals. Jason still wore his favorite paint-splattered work shirt and torn jeans. Cliff sported a Hawaiian shirt with a frayed collar and running shorts.

They were all so engrossed in their separate discussions, none of them even looked up when she stepped through the door.

It seemed odd to find they hadn't changed. Jan felt like years had gone by since she'd come into her great-uncle's money. While she was comfortably set for life, her old friends were still squeezing their pennies to get by.

And they were happy doing so. Like she had once been.

Jan couldn't say that her financial windfall had improved her life. At times she was sure having money had destroyed it. She hoped that it was just a temporary state of affairs, though. Once the mysteries of running L'Amour became clear, she could return to her old life. Or a semblance of it. She just had to get through this intern period before she could be happy again.

"You know what we need?" Angie demanded, still unaware that Jan stood off to the side. "A going-away party for Lloyd and Sandy."

"Yeah," Cliff agreed. "A real blowout, Lloyd.

Invite your friends and all the clients. Dazzle them with your good fortune."

"With this weather, it should be a barbecue," Jason insisted. "Maybe I could talk to Lotty about organizing one."

Jan felt her hackles rise at his mention of Charlotte Penn. In many ways, it hadn't been Simon's money that had changed her life, but the wealthy woman from Indianapolis. Charlotte had stepped in and taken over, not only in Jan's own life, but in that of her friends as well.

Let Charlotte throw a party for Lloyd and Sandy Amour? Like hell! The woman had hogged enough glory already between her promises to Jason and Cliff. There would be a picnic, but it would be planned and arranged by someone who was honestly fond of the Amours.

Jan squared her shoulders and strode across the room. Her heels clicked on the cement floor, the sound echoing in the vast space. "That's a great idea, Ange," she said brightly. "I was thinking the same thing." Jan beamed around at her friends. "If we all do the calls, we could round everyone up for a giant outdoor party at my house this Sunday, couldn't we?"

On Sunday morning Doug lay in a motel bed, 220 miles away in Effington, Indiana. The air conditioner droned, spilling cool air into the room. The blackout drapes kept the sun from disturbing his slumber.

But there were other things that could keep a man from sleeping. Like realizing he was in love.

Hell. He hadn't wanted to fall again. Or perhaps he merely meant *this soon*.

Doug punched at his pillows, stared at the ceiling, and tried to think logically.

In the last two weeks he'd driven the width of two states, from the edge of West Virginia all the way to a hamlet in eastern Illinois. He'd looked at property along Route 40, both new places and old. The older sites still appealed to him the most. There had been two or three definite possibilities. He would have to investigate them further, make offers, and see what happened.

Things with Jan wouldn't be that simple. But he couldn't put off facing her any longer. He missed Jan too much.

The travel clock on the bedside showed it was barely six. The coffee shop would be open. He could catch a quick breakfast, down a gallon of coffee, and be back in Richmond in four hours. Three if he ignored the speed limit.

What happened once he got back, though? Did he offer his heart and hand? Or did he only begin to find the woman Jan Ingraham was? Or the one she was becoming?

That was the crux. He was in love with the woman she'd been. If that woman no longer existed, what would his next move be?

The Jan he wanted didn't wear business suits, didn't run a graphics company. Doug dreamed of getting her to cut loose from·L'Amour, of working alongside her. Jan would be involved in her crafts, he with his sculptures. They would be the perfect couple, adaptable to each other's suggestions, each prepared to follow the other's muse if necessary. And there would be the gallery to support them.

At least Doug hoped it would.

Now that the whole idea of the gallery was actually beginning to come together, he was excited. It would be a permanent exhibition of various artists and craftspeople. The difference would be that this exhibit didn't move. It would be an extension of the portfolios Jan and her art-show friends had made for each other. A place where they could display their work, could sell their work. A place where interior decorators could find reasonable, original art. To stock the gallery, Jan's connections within the local art market would be a plus. Doug still had to meet and get to know the artists. Once the gallery was filled, he would promote it to the home decor firms of Ohio and Indiana. Would extend the advertising into larger cities around the country. He had made contacts in New York. They could be stretched to include Chicago, Miami, Los Angeles. His plans were far-reaching. But it could be done. He was betting his life savings— his future on it. All that was needed were the artists and a catalog of their work. As a graphics artist he'd be able to cut costs on producing a full-color advertising supplement. He'd do his own mechanical pasteups, costs could be trimmed and, if necessary, he'd photograph the artwork himself.

Doug had wanted to have things settled about the property before he said anything to Jan. Now he was no longer sure that waiting was the sensible thing to do.

The longer he delayed, the farther Jan slipped into her new persona. It wasn't too late to salvage the woman he loved. All he had to do was pry her away from Amour Graphics.

As soon try to leap over the moon.

It was going on eleven when Doug reached the lane that led to Jan's farmhouse.

At one time the clapboard building had sat in solitary splendor surrounded by fields. Now the farmland was nearly gone, swallowed up by new housing developments. The past was disappearing. All that remained was Jan's place.

It was set apart from the modern rat race. Instead of a dinky front yard, a good half acre of land stretched between Jan's cozy front porch and the road. It wasn't a neat carpet of green but a field of dull beige splotched with untamed color. *Weeds,* the neighbors probably called it. But he was almost sure that Jan would term the natural growth *materials*.

The plants weren't tall and had an evenness that argued regular care. Briefly, Doug wondered if she conned Jason or Clifford into wielding a sickle to keep it trimmed. Or did she do the cutting herself?

Somehow the second idea seemed closer to the truth. Jan wasn't the type of person to lean on her friends unless it was an emergency. She was much more inclined to do them favors.

Like buying a company she didn't need.

Doug followed the gravel drive, taking the fork that led to the back of the house. If things went well, he wouldn't be leaving that evening. Why broadcast his presence to the eagle-eyed neighbors?

Music spilled from the open windows. Kenny Loggins was insisting everyone celebrate him home. A pleasant female voice wailed along with him. Doug wasn't surprised that Jan hadn't heard him drive up, even though his tires had made the gravel spit. She was singing at the top of her lungs. The window fans were going at full speed. It would have taken a brass band to get Jan's attention.

Doug got out of his car and followed the sound of her voice into the kitchen.

She was cooking again, turning the house into an oven. The stove top was covered with large pans. On the counter nearby were plates heaped high with fried chicken. Still more cut-up fryers waited to be cooked. The smell of baking bread added to the heavenly scents in the room.

Jan sat at her huge kitchen table peeling boiled potatoes. Her movements were smooth as she skinned each one then dropped it in a large bowl of water. At the opposite end of the table, a pile of carrots, stalks of celery, bunches of radishes, and sprigs of green onions awaited her knife.

With the fans going and the music pitched at a deafening level, Jan still hadn't heard him.

Doug stood close to the screen door drinking in the picture she presented. Her hair was a tumble of dark curls. She wore a midriff-skimming top the color of spring leaves. When she stretched to drop another peeled potato in the bowl, Doug was treated to a view of lightly tanned skin. White athletic shorts completed her outfit, baring her legs in an incredibly long, luscious display that ended at her bare feet.

She didn't look like the woman who now owned L'Amour. She looked like the woman he loved.

Jan didn't bother to glance over her shoulder when someone thumped at her back door. "Come on in!" she shouted, and continued working. Jan hoped that Angie or Cliff or Jason had taken pity on her and decided to give her a helping hand.

It still rankled that no one had jumped to offer their services for the party. It was a great idea, they all declared. But help? They had all faded away from the suggestion.

Jan realized the root of the problem when she thought back. In the past they'd always planned the get-togethers as a team. This time there had been no discussion, none of the camaraderie that had everyone chipping in, bringing their specialties for a potluck. This time she had said the wrong thing and widened the gulf that had begun to form between her old friends and herself. She had *announced* that there would be a party at her house. From then on, that's all it had been. *Her* party at *her* house.

When pressed, the old team had made a few calls inviting people to come in honor of Lloyd and Sandy, then they'd drifted out of the L'Amour office. There had been no answer when she tried to get hold of them by phone later. So Jan had shouldered the responsibility and contacted everyone.

With guest list in hand, she'd figured out how much food was needed, and had ended up calling Walter to advance her some money from Simon's estate. She had spent nearly all of it at the grocery store. They might not be willing to chip in and help, but she was determined not to let her former friends find fault with this party. There would be enough food to feed half the town!

To save time she'd bought the chickens already cut up. The keg of beer was chilling in a tub of ice. Coolers lined the porch, filled with a variety of soft drinks. She made numerous gallon jugs of iced tea and lemonade the evening before, and set the bread to rise. At dawn she started cooking the chicken, frying it to a golden brown. While it simmered, Jan popped the waiting loaves of bread in the oven, and began work on the potato salad. The party was set for two o'clock. Jan just hoped that she managed to finish everything by then. There were still the finger foods to prepare, the chip dip to mix, the plastic dinnerware to get out, the paper plates to unwrap, the . . .

The knocking at the door was repeated. "Come on in!" Jan yelled, surprised that whoever it was hadn't entered on their own, and went on peeling potatoes.

"Don't tell me," Doug shouted close to her ear to be heard over the music, "you've branched out to the catering business now."

Jan nearly sliced off a piece of her thumb in surprise. She dropped the knife, the potato, and all intention of being mad at him. She jumped to her feet and was in his arms, right where she'd wanted to be for the last two weeks.

Doug didn't waste time saying hello. His mouth slanted hungrily over hers. His kiss was a greeting, a message, and a promise all wrapped in one. Jan responded with relish, pressing close to him.

On the stereo, Loggins ran out of steam. The

tape clicked off. In the blessed silence, Doug heard Jan give a sigh of pleasure. So he kissed her even more ardently.

"God, I missed you," he said when they parted.

"Ditto," Jan whispered. "Why did you go away?"

"Had to. I thought." His hand moved beneath her blouse, coasting up the curve of her spine. Her skin was like warm satin, but it didn't compare to the glow in those huge sky blue eyes of hers. Doug felt like a wanderer who had finally found his home.

"What's going on here?" he asked, his nod taking in the pile of chicken, the steaming stove, and the heaps of vegetables.

Jan sighed contentedly, her head nestled against his shoulder, her arms linked around his torso. "Catering, I guess. I'm throwing a going-away party for Lloyd and Sandy this afternoon."

Doug eyed the masses of food. "Invite the whole town?"

"Nearly."

"Where's the crew? Are Jase and the others bringing things over or are we about to be invaded by a team of inept cooks?" He really didn't want to share her just yet.

"Nope. They considered themselves guests, not workers."

Doug's mood took an abrupt swing. After all she'd done for them, buying L'Amour, shoulder-

ing the business end of the shop . . . the in-
grates! "The hell they did. And you let them?"

Jan blinked at the underlying violence of his
statement. "I didn't really have a choice."

He released her, looked around the kitchen
once more. "You sure as hell did, sugar. If they
want to work at L'Amour in the future, they
damn well better dance to your tune."

Jan sank back down in her chair and picked
up her knife and potato. "They're my friends,"
she said simply.

Which closed that discussion irrefutably, he realized. "Well, I'm not looking for a handout,
Jan. Tell me what you want me to do?"

She glanced up, surprised at his offer. Jason
and Cliff would have been content to sit at the
table and watch her work. "Help?"

Doug held up his hands, fingers splayed.
"Been known to enter a kitchen and emerge un-
scathed," he said. "See, all fingers intact."

She knew quite well that they were intact. And
just what they could do, working magic in the
comfort of her bed.

Before Jan could answer, the oven timer
buzzed. She put down her knife and went to the
stove. When three freshly baked loaves of bread
were cooling on the sideboard, she popped three
more in the heat and closed the door carefully.
Before she left the stove, she lifted the frying
pan lids and turned the sizzling chicken over.

If being a good cook had been a requirement

186

for gaining Doug's soul, Jan would have succeeded. The heavenly scents from her kitchen would have sealed his fate as firmly as a contract with the devil.

"Why, may I ask, did you bake bread when there is so much more to be done?" he asked, leaning against the counter. "Why not buy it in nice neat plastic bags?"

Jan twisted the timer switch, setting it once again. "Because it's my specialty. Everyone would be expecting it."

Doug frowned. Jan did too much just because it was expected of her. As a result her so-called friends took advantage of her. Well, he wouldn't be one of them. A freeloader for her affection.

"I think they would all have survived quite well on store-bought," he insisted.

Jan set the timer down and moved over to where a batch of bread awaited her attention. "You only say that because you haven't tasted it," she said with a grin and cut a crusty slice. Her head cocked to one side, almost like a bird, watching him. "Butter? Jam?"

The aroma of fresh-baked bread was heady stuff, but so was the tender, flirtatious expression on her lovely face.

"Don't tell me that you churned the butter yourself and put up the jam, too." He wouldn't have put it past her.

Jan laughed. "Of course not. I've never done

187

either. Now if we were talking about apple butter . . ."

"Apple butter," Doug repeated. He accepted the unadorned slice of bread she passed him.

"I do make that," Jan confessed, and actually blushed. "In the fall. But I used the last of it for breakfast last week. As soon as the new harvest is in, I'll make you some."

Doug bit into the bread. It was heaven. It surpassed the celestial smell that blanketed the kitchen. He sighed in pleasure. "Marry me," he said.

Jan giggled. "I've heard that one before. What is it with you men and your stomachs? It's just bread."

And a lot of work on her part. Didn't she understand that? Now she wanted to make him apple butter, too.

"I'm serious," Doug said. "Marry me."

"Sure you are," she murmured, her voice still wavering toward a second giggle. "If you want to help, what's your preference? Potato salad or nibble salad? And, before I get back to work, what's your choice of music? I've got Glenn Frey, Kenny Loggins, Michael McDonald, Mister Mister, Breathe. . . ."

Chapter Eleven

When the list of singers and groups was complete, Doug chose Richard Marx simply because it was the only name he could remember. With the strains of "Keep Coming Back" filling the farmhouse, Doug settled at the opposite end of the table and began hacking away at the carrots. It was the perfect song, he thought. Unlike all the other women in his past, Jan Ingraham was the only one whom he could ever picture himself repeatedly coming back to.

Too bad he'd blown it. Would she ever believe he'd meant that spontaneous proposal? That he was serious about marriage? Probably not.

Working in the kitchen with her was a very companionable way to pass a Sunday. Doug had a few ideas on how to improve on it. Like starting the day with a lazy morning in bed *without* the hefty Sunday newspaper.

While they both peeled vegetables, Jan told him about her meetings with L'Amour clients and with her great-uncle's lawyer. Doug described the properties he'd visited, trying to paint them in the rosiest possible terms. After all, he wanted her to live in one of them with him. A good bit of PR never hurt.

"Think you could help me make the final decision on a place?" he asked carefully casual. "You know. Give me a woman's opinion."

Jan had moved from potatoes to chopping onions. Her eyes looked teary but her voice was still cheerful. "With Lloyd leaving this week, I don't see how I can get away. I mean, it's nice that he trusts me for the money since the probate isn't finished yet on Uncle Simon's will. The paperwork's all done though, so Lloyd and Sandy are anxious to begin their retirement. But it also sticks me with details for the graphics jobs Lloyd lined up. He had a real burst of energy going, too. We'll be swamped trying to get things done by the deadlines."

Doug finished scraping the last of the four pounds of carrots and began chopping celery. "I'd offer my services, sugar, but I've got my own seeds sown. Besides," he added, lightly. "I just proposed to you and I'd hate to think you'd suddenly accept just to wheedle graphics work out of me." Hopefully that took the sting out of his refusal. But there was no way he was ever crossing the threshold of Amour Graphics again. Unless it was to carry her off.

Which it was beginning to look like he'd have to do.

Jan wiped onion tears away with the back of

her hand. "That's okay. While it isn't what they prefer to be doing, Jason, Cliff, and even Angie have pulled their weight on graphics before. From what I've seen of the contracts, it's rather lightweight stuff, nearly copy ready from the account."

She finished dicing the last onion and reached for the potatoes again, cutting them in half-inch cubes. "If we keep our nose to the grindstone, maybe I can swing a weekend though," Jan offered.

That sounded hopeful. "Next weekend?"

She finished a potato, her brow slightly furrowed in thought. She looked so adorable he wanted to forget the damn going-away party and spend the day making love to her.

The timer buzzed again. Jan put her work aside, returned to the stove and removed the current batch of fried chicken from the skillets. "I'm not sure," she said. "It depends on a lot of things." She dropped a new piece of chicken in a bag of seasoned flour and shook it. When the thigh was sizzling in the skillet, she repeated the process with a leg. "Weekend after would be better."

Progress was being made, Doug decided. "It's a date, then. Just you and me, alone for forty-eight hours."

Jan kept on shaking her bag of chicken pieces, but she grinned back over her shoulder at him. "Think you can stand me that long?"

Doug stretched in his chair, easing the stiffness in his shoulders. "Sugar," he murmured tenderly, "I thought I'd made that clear. Eternity wouldn't be too long to share with you."

Flowery words. Why did men think you had to hear them? Or more to the point, why did they say them and never mean them?

She'd take the forty-eight hours with pleasure and let eternity take care of itself. Other men she'd dated had been prone to mention that infinite stretch of time, but managed to shorten it to a couple pages of the calendar. Doug MacLeod would be the same.

Jan had showered and changed into a peach and pink flowered sundress by the time the first guests arrived. Besides the L'Amour clients, the Amours's friends, and the employees of L'Amour's rival firms, a squadron of flies and wasps and an army of ants flew or marched in to join the fun. While arms waved warding off the pests, plates were filled, then refilled. The usual compliments were made about Jan's homemade bread, as well as a few sly remarks made about Doug's presence and the way he moved familiarly around Jan's house. But for the most part the attention centered on Lloyd and Sandy Amour.

When the sun set, the crowd lingered on, enjoying the cool night air. Dropping with fatigue,

Jan wished they would all go away. Instead, she found herself trapped by Clifford.

"Any more beer, Jannie?"

From the look of his bloodshot eyes, Cliff had drunk more than his fair share. Fortunately, he'd arrived with the newlyweds, and Angie's husband, the designated driver, had been sticking to iced tea all day. "There might be a few of the Strohs Doug brought over a few weeks ago in the frig yet."

Cliff's brows rose in theatrical surprise. "Doug's, huh. You two are pretty cozy, aren't you."

Jan wondered if it was because she was tired that her hackles rose at his tone. Cliff seemed to be implying that the situation was unusual, that there was a reason other than a mutual attraction involved.

"We enjoy each other's company, if that's what you're asking, Bogen," she snapped.

"Jannie, Jannie, Jannie," he protested. "I'm an old friend, remember?"

He hadn't been acting like it lately, she thought. But maybe it wasn't her friends' attitude that had changed. Maybe it was hers.

"The least you could have done is give me first whack at the fortune," Cliff said.

Jan stiffened. Held her breath.

Cliff's voice dropped to a new, intimate level. "I figured that Jase deserved to make a move before I did. But he's got Charlotte tied up and

193

in the bag. He doesn't need your money now. But why'd you turn to his ole buddy from school though? What's he got that I haven't?"

Jan's hands clenched. She counted to ten to control the flare of temper that threatened to engulf her. "What are you talking about?"

Her voice was a low-pitched hiss, but Cliff didn't seem affected by it. "About MacLeod, 'course," he insisted. "Hell, Jannie, you know there's nothing wrong with a man letting a woman pay the bills, especially when it lets him follow his muse. I'd be sufficiently grateful, you know. Write you love poems. Dedicate a screen-play to you . . ."

Jan's sight blurred. No wonder Doug hadn't wanted her to buy L'Amour. He had been making plans for her money all along.

No, that couldn't be true. He'd invited her to see the old coaching houses before Aunt Beatrice had arrived. But he'd argued against her wishes after Bea had made her announcement. Men from New York City moved fast, and didn't let the grass grow over any opportunity.

That's definitely what she was. A ticket to a life of ease. He'd had a fiancée in the city, Jan recalled. Jason had told them all about his college roommate's lifestyle and accomplishments before Doug had ever arrived in town. Perhaps the fiancée had found Doug favored her fortune more than her form and broke things off.

To top it off, he'd conveniently played her

194

along for the last couple of weeks. Reeling her in as if she were a damn fish! He'd made love to her. Exquisitely. Then disappeared. Only those teasing, lovelorn-sounding phone messages had kept her primed. Ready for him to reenter the scene that morning.

And propose to her.

Damn! The bastard!

Jan yanked open her refrigerator and rooted at the back for the remaining bottles of beer. She'd hidden them so the guests wouldn't help themselves. But Cliff deserved a reward for helping her to avoid disaster.

It was the last reward or favor he'd get from her. Imagine, thinking he could take the leap from buddy to lover. And just because her great-uncle had cursed her with money!

Cliff stumbled back out of the house, leaving Jan alone in the shambles of her kitchen. Not for long, however.

Doug caught the screen door before it had closed and pulled it open again. "God is kind," he said in a teasing voice. "The first of the crowd are taking their leave. Better get out there, madam hostess. I'll see if I can repair any of the damage in here."

"Don't bother," she snapped. "Leave it."

He looked at her closely. Put his hands on her bare arms and peered down into her face. "Everything all right, Jan?"

Lord! Why did he have to sound so tender,

look so sincere? At least now she knew he was lying with every word.

Jan got a grip on herself. She couldn't let him know she'd stumbled on his game plan. "Just tired," she mumbled. "I'd better go shake a few hands."

Doug smiled.

Damn, why did her heart have to contract just at the sight? She'd told herself repeatedly that he was just passing through. That no matter what he said, there was no future for them. There never had been with other men who'd babbled the same sentiments in the aftermath of passion. But to hear those empty promises just because she'd inherited the better part of Simon's estate. . . . Lord, what a fool she was!

"Cheer up," Doug urged. "Maybe the early birds will start a trend and soon everybody will be gone and we can be alone."

Of course he'd think that. She'd been melting beneath the look in his gray eyes all day. Jan glanced up at him. There was passion brewing in his eyes now, making them dark and mysteriously alluring.

"I'm awfully tired," she murmured.

"I'll revitalize you," Doug promised, planted a light kiss on her forehead and turned Jan toward the door.

By the time the last guest had driven off, Jan

knew exactly what to do. She was going to play along. For a while.

She was amazed to find her kitchen in nearly perfect order. Granted, some of the things weren't quite where she would have put them. But whenever Jase and the others had helped, nothing had been put back where it belonged either.

Doug greeted her with a glass of wine. "We never got to drink this, remember?" he asked and gave her his lazy Stark Savage grin.

"I remember," Jan said.

He urged her to take a sip, then kissed her lingeringly.

Play along, Jan reminded herself and swayed toward him. It really wasn't hard. His lips were tart with wine, as sensuous as velvet as they drifted lightly across hers. He teased and tempted in the caress. Made it easy for Jan to forget, temporarily, that he was a fortune hunter.

Doug entwined his fingers with hers and led Jan back into the living room. The lamp was turned to the lowest setting, just as she had once arranged it. Doug settled down on the sofa, pulling her down on his lap.

It was impossible to resist when she wanted nothing more than to be in his arms. Carefully balancing her glass of wine in one hand, Jan curled the other behind his neck. Her fingertips brushed lightly through his hair. So soft, so wavy. So . . .

Jan buried her hand deeper, slanted her mouth over his.

It was a game, after all. Two could deceive as easily as one.

"Mmm, nice," Doug murmured.

He nuzzled her throat. Jan closed her eyes, fighting back waves of longing. They lapped at her anger as if determined to wash the memory of Clifford's words away. She almost wished that they would, that she could return to the euphoria of earlier. Could believe once more that Doug MacLeod might fall in love with her.

"What should we drink to? Us?" he asked.

With his mouth against her skin, warm, damp, and insistent, it was difficult to think. It wasn't just Doug's lips that caressed her. Just the sound of his deep, mellow voice did things to Jan, enveloping her in a cocoon of sensation.

It sounded sacrilegious to agree to his toast considering she had no intention of there ever being an *us*. "To your coaching house," Jan suggested and raised her glass. "May you find the right property."

"With your help, I'm sure I will."

Yeah, sure, she thought. *My money's staying far away from it, buddy.*

"I've been thinking about that weekend of ours," he said. "Rather than just look at more

198

houses, why don't we do something really special?"

"Such as?" Jan prompted, wondering if there were dollar signs attached to the proposition.

He put his wineglass aside on the end table and nuzzled her ear. "San Francisco," Doug murmured. "City by the Bay. Pretty romantic spot, sugar."

There were two distinct parts of her, Jan decided. One was the cool mind, the part of her that knew what he was up to and made sly remarks to counter each of his smooth phrases. Then there was that other part, which not only ate up every word, but sent sensations rippling through her body until it tingled everywhere he touched her. And now that Doug had both hands free, there didn't seem to be a spot he intended to miss.

"Expensive," she purred. Damn it, she was nearly panting! A little more self-control was needed. Jan moved back from Doug, ostensibly to take another sip of wine.

"My treat," he whispered, his tongue tracing erotic little circles around her ear now.

Jan was trying to fight down the rush of pleasure that threatened to envelop her. "The will isn't through probate yet. I'm still broke. Especially after this party," she said before his words penetrated her consciousness. Jan turned sharply. *"What did you say?"*

Doug pried her fingers from around the wineglass and set it next to his. "I said I was footing the bill," he said. "You seem awfully jumpy tonight, Jan."

"It's just that I . . . I . . ." She was babbling. Making a fool of herself. Damn it! She was a businesswoman now. She couldn't let people, especially not men, manipulate her. Of course he was paying for the trip. It was all part of the plan to lure her into trusting him. Surely if Charlotte Penn could spot a man who was ready for marriage, a man like Douglas MacLeod could read the same susceptibility in her. He obviously knew she had been on the brink of falling in love with him. Emphasis on *had been,* the sane part of her mind insisted. But that other self, the one that searched for sensation, was ready to argue. *What was it with this* had-been *jazz?* She was in love with him, had been from the first. Ever since the moment he'd kissed her when they posed for the cover of Charlotte's book.

"Just that you what?" Doug asked, his voice husky.

Jan found she was lying back on the sofa, her arms around his neck. "That I'm tired," she said. "It's been a long, busy day."

Doug dropped a light kiss on her lips. "Then let's go to bed. Want me to carry you again?"

Jan fought down the temptation. There was romance and then there was *romance,* her sensible self argued. Be mercenary, but don't be stupid.

"I'll walk this time." She regretted the words as soon as they were said. Perhaps that was because Doug was now concentrating on the sensitive hollow of her throat though. It had to be!

"About San Francisco," Doug said. "I'll get the tickets, book the hotel, see about reservations for a show." He ticked off the items quickly, as if they were things on a grocery list. "Ever been there, sugar?"

"No, but I—"

"You'll love the place," Doug promised. "Now about that bed . . ." His hands ran slowly down her body doing delicious things to her senses.

Damn it all, Jan's common sense swore. Why did he have to have such talented fingers? It was her last sensible thought of the night.

Doug left Richmond a couple of days later to continue investigating National Road properties. Jan was almost glad to see him leave.

Almost.

Part of her was not looking forward to sleeping alone again. He hadn't come to Amour Graphics but each evening he'd come to visit her at the farmhouse. And had stayed through breakfast coffee. Jan hadn't been able to find it in herself to act cool toward Doug. She excused herself on the basis that sex was an addicting

201

form of exercise. She would think of his visits as part of a brief, glittering affair, nothing more. Certainly it would be disastrous to term it love when she was sure that it was nothing of the sort for Doug.

Now that he was gone again, she could begin accomplishing things.

Exactly what those things were, Jan wasn't sure. There was probably a list of them somewhere. All she had to do was find it. Probably on her desk at L'Amour.

L'Amour.

When had she last been eager to go to the graphics shop? It hadn't been in a good while, that was for sure. Now it was a chore to get dressed and drive to her business. That hadn't been what she wanted. It was supposed to be a pleasure to go to work. Especially to a place where she'd planned to spend so many happy hours working with her friends.

Angie was the only one at work when Jan reached Amour Graphics. The blonde was hunched over the computer keyboard. Although there were sheets of copy at her side to be re-set, Angie wasn't feeding anything onto the disk.

Jan was only partway across the room when Angie dashed out of her chair. Her face was a distinct green as she headed for the restroom.

Jan followed, her expression alternating between concern for her friend and worry that the missing members of the team had succumbed to the same malady. The noises issuing from behind the closed door sounded distinctly like those made by a person suffering from food poisoning. And the day before, Jan had brought in all the leftovers from the party for a smorgasbord lunch.

"Ange!" Jan called through the door. "Are you all right? Should I call a doctor?"

The door swung open. Despite her pasty complexion, Angie's lips curved in a wry smile. "It's nothing, Jan. I'm just going to have a baby."

"A baby!" Everything Jan knew about pregnancy raced through her mind. "But you haven't even been married a month yet. You don't get morning sickness this soon." As if that would make a difference to Angie's stomach.

"This soon?" Angie's smile widened. Her color began returning. "Jannie, honey, I'm nearly two months gone. Why do you think I got married so fast?"

Jan leaned back against the wall, stunned at her friend's casual confession. "How did it happen?"

Angie's look changed to one of derision. "If you don't know, you better stop having those sleepovers with MacLeod."

Jan glared. She straightened up. "You know what I mean. I thought you were taking precautions."

"I was," Angie said. "Until I realized I was never going to get married unless I got a little help."

"But that's blackmail!"

Angie shrugged. "It worked, didn't it? And I wanted to have a baby."

The whole plan disgusted Jan. How could Angie announce such perfidy so calmly, as if it were an everyday occurrence. Like taking out the trash!

"Are you going to be all right?" Jan asked, her tone a bit cooler than it had been.

"Yes," Angie announced and took a step out of the doorway. Almost immediately her skin turned a sickly green. "No," she said and turned back into the room.

No longer in sympathy with the woman—she was obviously not the friend Jan had thought her—Jan stalked back to the front office and dialed Clifford. He picked up the phone on the first ring.

"Could you come in and get the type set on the Lowry project?" Jan asked. "When you're finished you could work on your screenplay."

Once that would have been all the carrot that was needed. "No can do," Cliff said. "Charlotte gave me the manuscript of *Passion's Last Stand* to read so I could write the movie version. You'll never believe this, Jannie, but it's good. Damn good. And you know why? Because it's pure farce! It's a satire of the historical romance novel. It's great!"

Just what she needed. Another Charlotte Penn supporter.

"Listen, Cliff, the copy won't take but an hour or so, if that. You could begin working on the screen version this afternoon, blocking scenes, that sort of thing," Jan suggested, dropping one of the phrases he'd used when talking about his dream.

"I'd like to help you, Jannie, but I don't need the computer at the shop anymore. Charlotte advanced me money to work on the script. I bought my own computer with some of it, a more up-to-date model than you've got at L'Amour. I'm going to move into a bigger place, too, so I'll have an office to work in at home."

Charlotte. Jan growled the name when she hung up the phone. She dialed another number.

It took six rings for Jason to answer.

"I know it isn't in your normal line to key in the copy," Jan began, "but Angie's sick and Cliff is tied up. Please, Jase, could you come in? I'd do it myself but I'm booked solid with Lloyd's appointments yet."

Jason sighed deeply. "Hell, Jannie, you know if I keyed the copy, everything would have to be redone anyway. Call Doug," he suggested and hung up before she could comment.

Friends. Jan's temper simmered.

"Jannie?" Angie's voice didn't sound quite as

205

peppy as usual. "I think I'd better go home. The doctor told me I had to take it easy right now."

Jan drummed her fingers on the desktop. "I've heard that Chinese peasant women give birth in the fields and keep on working," she said.

"I'm a little more delicate," Angie replied. "I'll call you at home tomorrow if I don't feel any better."

Jan watched the blonde drive away then walked into the vast emptiness of the workroom. What had happened to the plans they'd all made? Jason had wanted a decent-sized studio. She could still see him pacing off the area he'd planned to convert to his own use. Clifford had wanted an office separate from his home so that he could concentrate on his scripts. Had wanted to use the computer at L'Amour to concoct his screenplays. Now Charlotte had made that unnecessary. Angie had just wanted a steady income and the time to watch her soaps. Apparently she planned to watch them from the comfort of her bed, milking her "delicate" condition for all it was worth.

Her footsteps echoing in the space, Jan moved to the corner she'd planned to use for her crafts. She could almost picture the shelves of materials, the pegs on which to hang wreaths, the boxes in which to store the dough ornaments. Her dream wouldn't materialize here

206

either, for now she'd lost the time to devote to her creations.

Slowly, Jan moved back to her desk in the front office. The desk that had once belonged to Lloyd Amour. She flipped through the Rolodex that had once been Sandy Amour's. The call to the temporary employment agency was accomplished quickly. While she was waiting for them to call back with the name of the receptionist they would be sending, Jan dialed her first two appointments and rescheduled them for later in the day.

She sighed. *Friends*. The word left a bitter taste in Jan's mouth.

Chapter Twelve

Doug felt like he'd been caught in a hurricane without ever seeing the calm in the center. Perhaps that was yet to come. In the past seven days he'd inspected the three most promising properties looking for minute problems. He'd talked wood rot, termites, and tornado insurance. He'd studied the time droop of ceilings, the antique plumbing, and the ancient electrical wiring. He'd paced off each square foot of surrounding land and dickered over prices. But in the end he decided he couldn't wait any longer and he'd closed the deal on the sweetest little coaching house along the whole route. Located halfway between Richmond, Indiana, and Englewood, Ohio, the property consisted of ten acres of land, and boasted a wild spinney, a decent-sized barn, and flat land next to the house that could be turned into a parking lot for the gallery.

A litany of things to be done to the place ran through Doug's head. The last owner had destroyed the look of the building by installing aluminum siding. It would be one of the first things to go. What was the use of owning a historic house if it didn't maintain its original look? The wood flooring would have to be sanded down and refinished, the plaster walls patched and repainted. The fireplaces would have to be cleaned and loose stonework replaced. The ancient-looking furnace in the dirt-floored basement definitely had to go. And soon. Doug wanted to move into the place the day the title papers came through. Sooner if possible.

Fortunately it was a short drive to Richmond, half an hour at most. If Jan didn't weaken during the romantic "honeymoon" he planned in San Francisco, he could continue his courtship, luring her to the coach house.

She was the reason he'd finally chosen this particular site, the reason he'd folded during the negotiations and paid more than he'd originally offered. But this property would give Jan a reason to seek him out. He now owned a full acre of private woodland well stocked with the natural materials she favored.

Once the house was in order, the lower level arranged for his gallery, the upper for his personal quarters, he'd attack the barn. Wide picture windows could be installed at the loft level for his studio. When he convinced Jan to move in, the old tack room would convert to her work area with adjacent storage in the stalls. His long-term plan was to remodel the rest of the barn into a home. The tiny rooms above the gallery just weren't sufficient space for a family.

Was there something about a man buying land and loving a very special woman that made him think more about the future? Not just the immediate future, but the long-span future. His land had been cleared by a pioneer nearly two centuries ago, and had been passed on to that man's sons and grandsons. Before heading back to Richmond, Doug stood on his newly purchased property and found he wanted in on that chain of immortality. He wanted to bequeath this place to his sons, and their sons.

And he wanted Janelle Ingraham to help him begin the new chain to the future.

The highway sign welcoming him back to Indiana swept by in a blur. From habit, Doug took the exit and turnings that would bring him to Amour Graphics. It was still early afternoon. Jan would be at the shop rather than at home. With all the little jobs Lloyd had lined up for the firm before leaving, the place would be humming with activity as Jason worked on pen and ink illustrations for a local cabinetmaker, Clifford set his hand to advertising copy, and

Angie did whatever it was Angie usually did. There had also been a logo to be developed for a dry cleaner's, a flier for a community theater presentation, and stationery to be designed for a law firm. Knowing Jan's business was running smoothly, and that she herself would be swamped doing the pasteups, Doug had resorted to messages on her answering machine again. He'd settled on the property closest to Richmond, but the other two possibilities had been at opposite ends of the route, one just west of the Ohio River not far from Wheeling, West Virginia, the other in Illinois near Martinsville.

When he hadn't been prowling over the respective houses and land, he'd been behind the wheel driving from one location to the other.

That was behind him now. And the weekend in San Francisco with Jan lay directly ahead. They were booked on a plane out of the Dayton airport late the next afternoon, a direct flight that would get them into San Francisco early in the evening. There would be little time to settle into their room at the Hyatt Regency on the Embarcadero before leaving for the show at the Fairmont, the historic hotel atop Nob Hill. Afterwards, he'd make sure Jan was treated to the romantic view of the city and the bay from The Top of the Mark.

If things went as he planned, Jan would realize he hadn't been flippant in proposing to her.

211

He'd been serious.

He took the turns along side streets to avoid rush hour traffic. Something that couldn't be avoided even in Richmond. But when Doug pulled into the lot next to L'Amour, he found Jan's new dark blue Oldsmobile was the only occupant.

Inside a stranger faced him.

"Welcome to Amour Graphics. Can I help you?" asked a pert older woman. She wore a neat polyester suit, sensible pumps, and a wide smile. Her dark hair was highlighted with gray, cut short, teased, and sprayed to stay in place.

Feeling like he'd stepped into the wrong office, Doug pulled up short. "Jan Ingraham?"

The woman's smile changed slightly, her eyes softened. "You must be Mr. MacLeod," she said. "Ms. Ingraham is in the back. I don't think she's expecting you though."

"She's not," Doug agreed, and pushed through the swinging double doors into the workroom.

As he had suspected, Jan was alone. The radio was on softly, tuned to her favorite station. Phil Collins was crooning about another day in Paradise. Jan was hunched over the layout table, a jar of rubber cement at one hand, a T-square at the other. Around her lay the tools of her trade, an Exacto knife, rolls of adhesive-backed borderlines, sheets of set copy, photostats of completed art work.

"Hi," Doug said quietly.

Jan started, straightened, and turned slowly to face him. She leaned back against the table, her hands braced on the edges. "Hi," she echoed.

She looked lovely. And she looked like hell.

His eyes skimmed over her tousled dark brown curls, lingered unhappily on the deep circles beneath her eyes. A lackluster glaze dulled the usual brilliance of her eyes. They weren't the color of a clear summer sky now. They looked more like polluted ponds.

Doug crossed to Jan, ran his palms up her arms, and kissed her gently. She didn't return the caress. Didn't move from her stance against the table. He wondered if she could. She looked ready to drop.

"When's the last time you slept?" he asked.

She essayed a slight, wry smile. "Sleep? I think I caught an hour or two sometime in the last few days."

The phone in the outer office rang. The stranger answered it, her voice crisp and efficient. The professionalism of her manner sounded out of place at L'Amour. Funny that he should think so after trying to instill that attitude in the freelancers just a few weeks ago. Sandy Amour's greeting had always been friendly, and a bit like an eager puppy.

213

"Ms. Ingraham?" The woman pushed open one of the doors tentatively. "Bourne, Colleridge, and Handel are on the phone. They want to know if the letterhead samples are ready for their okay yet. You had promised them today."

Jan sighed loudly. "I'll have them at their office when it opens in the morning, Mrs. Fine. Please apologize for me. Again."

The older woman nodded and returned to her station.

"Mrs. Fine?" Doug jerked his head in the direction of the office.

"Temporary help agency. She's been a life-saver."

"What happened to the crew?"

Jan turned back to her work. "Mind if I work while we talk? I'm two days behind on deadlines already."

After the Penn Publishing assignment he'd sworn that he would never do another display — unless it was for the benefit of his gallery. Well, if a man was going to renege on promises, it was better to do so on those made only to himself. "Only if you let me help," Doug said. "What's next?"

Jan sighed again, this time the sound echoed with relief. "B. C. and H.'s letterheads. I haven't even begun on them yet. Lawyers. They want a corporate look, but don't want to be

214

stuffy. My notes are in that folder." She nodded toward a corner of the layout table.

Doug picked it up and leafed through the samples of the law firm's previous stationery and business cards. It was pretty staid stuff. "So where's Jase? Or Cliff, or Angie?"

Jan's hands moved, her motions efficient and sure as she completed the mechanical for an advertising flier. "Angie's pregnant, sick as a dog, and under the delusion that she's delicate. The woman has the constitution of a workhorse. She claims she's under doctor's orders to spend her time in bed—watching soap operas and eating chocolates, no doubt.

"Clifford is deep into his screenplay on *Passion's Last Stand.*"

Doug picked up a pencil and pad. He began sketching out ideas for B. C. and H. "You're kidding. What's he living on?"

"Charlotte's bounty, of course. She gave him a ridiculously large advance and the manuscript. He claims the book is a howl, that she's a master of satire. Personally, I think he's just kissing up," Jan said, her head still bent over her work.

"And Jason?"

Jan's teeth clenched but she kept working. The stat of a breakfront was pasted down, pried up, adjusted, and set again. "In training for star status," she snarled. "Charlotte's bought

215

a house, furnished it—nearly covering the walls with masterpieces from the brush of the Great Holloway—and is throwing a party in a couple of weeks to launch him. Guests to arrive from Indy, Chicago, even New York, for all I know. Jase doesn't have time for obscure little jobs anymore. He's groomed for fame."

"Hell," Doug said.

"You said it," Jan agreed. She straightened, stretched, her hands on her lower back.

"So they all deserted you when you needed them." Doug finished one rough design, ripped off the sheet of paper, and began another. "How many samples do you need?"

Jan rolled her head trying to ease the tension in her shoulder blades and neck. "Three will do. At the moment, I don't even care if they're good. I just want them done."

Doug's pencil continued to fly across the pad. "Oh, they'll be done, sugar. And they'll be more than good, they'll be damn good. So damn good you'll have to up the price for them."

"Your usual razzle-dazzle, Manhattan?" Her voice was tired and a bit brittle.

Doug wished he could coddle her. Could vanquish the tension in her face. "For a law firm?" he demanded, his eyebrows rising in theatrical shock before he dissolved into a wicked grin. "I'm tempering the dazzle, but the mock-ups will be slapped together in nothing flat. Have

216

to be. We're bound for San Francisco tomorrow, remember?"

"Oh, hell," Jan said. "Is it that weekend already? I guess I lost track of the days. There's too much to do here, Doug. I can't make it."

Doug went on working. She'd said it all too fast, as if the excuse had been well rehearsed. Why? Was she ticked off that he'd been gone? That he'd never called when she was home? Well, he wasn't going to let her off the hook. Not when Jan looked in urgent need of time away from L'Amour.

"What's left to do? Once the samples are done, the firm's got some time to ponder, right?" he asked, his tone carefully offhand.

"Right," she admitted reluctantly.

Doug nodded at the ad on the table before her. "Does that mechanical have to be proofed?"

"No," Jan said slowly. "They okayed it on the layout."

"Anything else?"

She rubbed her forehead. "Ah . . ."

Before she could invent another excuse, Doug changed the subject. "When's the last time you ate?"

Jan gave him a dirty look. "You're as bad as my mother."

Doug kept his eyes on the sketch as it filled

out with each stroke of the pencil. "That long," he mused.

Jan closed her eyes. She was too tired to bristle. Too tired to be mad. And just too damn glad that someone was helping with the layouts! Even if it was Doug.

"Mrs. Fine brought me back a sandwich when she went to lunch."

"Uh-huh." He sounded suspicious. "But you didn't eat it." He pointed with the eraser end of his pencil toward the neat cellophane package that protruded from beneath a stack of rejected copy.

So that's where it had gotten to! Jan shrugged. "So I forgot about it. Sue me."

"Not me, love. But B. C. and H. may if I don't get these mock-ups ready." Doug ripped another sheet from his pad and began a third sketch. "Too bad they don't have a motto or something. You know, 'Best Ambulance Chasers in Seven Counties.'"

"Or 'Wayne County's Finest'?"

"Naw," Doug said. "The police department probably fancies that title. Why don't we have pizza delivered? It's almost five. Utilize the magnificent Mrs. Fine to call in the order. Pepperoni and sausage?"

"Double cheese and black olives," Jan countered. Oh, it was so good to have someone to work along side her again. "Salad?"

218

He grinned up at her and received the ghost of her usual smile in return. "Absolutely," Doug declared. "And a large Coke. We'll finish this stuff off and go out for dessert afterwards."

It sounded delightful. Even if he was a fortune hunter, she'd been so lonely lately. A date with the devil would have looked good. "Okay, but only if it's hot fudge sundaes," Jan said.

Doug cringed. "After pizza?"

Jan's smile was stronger now. He was pleased to note there was even a slight bit more color in her cheeks. "Cast-iron stomach," she confessed.

"Probably a stomach pump for me," Doug said. "But what the heck." After all, Doug admitted, a man in love would do almost anything. Even guarantee himself indigestion.

As it turned out, his stomach didn't have to pass the test. Jan fell asleep with her head on the table while Doug converted his sketches into samples on the computer.

The next morning went by in a flurry of activity. Doug personally delivered the promised letterhead designs to Bourne, Colleridge, and Handel, then went off to the printers to leave the flier Jan had completed the evening before.

At the lawyers he "confessed" to a scowling Mr. Bourne that Ms. Ingraham had personally designed the samples with them in mind, rejecting a dozen other ideas as unworthy of such a prestigious firm. Bourne had looked startled, had glanced down at each of the three proof sheets, and looked gratified.

The printer wasn't as easily reconciled. The camera-ready layout had been due Thursday afternoon, not early Friday morning. They couldn't guarantee that the job would be finished by the time originally promised. Doug looked concerned, then resolute. They realized that Amour Graphics was under new management? he asked. Perhaps they didn't know that expansion was contemplated? It was the centrality of Richmond, within easy reach of the major cities, Indianapolis, Dayton, Columbus, Cincinnati, that had interested the new owners. There had been rumors that they had connections within NCR's Dayton headquarters. It would be a shame to have to find a new printer in the area when a major contract was signed.

Although the printer wouldn't commit himself to meeting the current deadline, he did look pensive when Doug left.

As he drove back to his apartment to pack for the West Coast trip, Doug wondered if any of his Scots ancestors had found their way across the Irish Sea and laid a smacker on the Blarney Stone. He'd never lied quite that slickly in his whole life. Another example of how love warped a man's concept of himself.

It was all worth it when he sat next to Jan on the plane and she announced out of the blue, "You were right. I never should have bought L'Amour."

The plane climbed higher into the clouds, quickly putting distance between itself and the tilled fields that surrounded the runways in Vandalia, Ohio, the site of the Dayton International Airport. Doug pressed back into his seat, his eyes on the glowing No Smoking/Fasten Seat Belts sign. He didn't need to be looking at Jan to know how lovely she looked in her blue chambray halter dress. Her bare shoulders were covered at the moment, hidden beneath the lightweight white cotton jacket she'd donned in the air-conditioned plane.

It wasn't just Jan's lovely shoulders that drew him. It was her overwhelming, giving nature. Now she was giving him a gift as well. The knowledge that she knew she was out of her depth as owner of Amour Graphics.

Doug tried to keep his voice casual. Inside he was whooping as if he'd made the winning touchdown, or hit a tie-breaking home run.

"How so?"

Jan kept her eyes on the patchwork of farms far beneath them. "It didn't quite work out, did it." She was quiet a bit longer. "I want to thank you for helping me. L'Amour would have lost those accounts but for you."

Ease into it, he told himself. *Don't rush. Think of the suggestion as if it were a seed. Wait for the right moment to plant it then let it germinate in its own good time.*

"Do you really want to hold on to them?"

Jan did glance over at him then. She gave a short cough of strangled laughter. "I can almost hear Great-Uncle Simon chuckling. But the truth is, there's a part of me that won't let L'Amour fail. I've contracted to pay good money for the business. I don't want to lose my investment. I want the shop to be profitable and yet I know I can't make it so. I'm a graphic artist, not a manager. There were two Amours, Lloyd and Sandy. I'm only one person. When everyone walked out on me, there was no one to cushion the fall."

Doug began to put his hand over hers, and thought better of it. "Not even me," he admitted quietly.

"You were there last night though. Sorry I fell asleep and didn't thank you for your help."

Doug watched her, wondering just where he stood with her. One moment he thought she returned his affection, that she was in love with him, or at least about to take the tumble that would land her in his arms. Now he wasn't so sure. The fact that she admitted her mistake over L'Amour didn't cheer him. It hurt her too much to give him any pleasure.

The Seat Belt sign dimmed and the stewardesses came around offering drinks and roasted nuts.

Doug crunched on the snack, his thoughts ahead at their destination. There was someone in San Francisco who just might save the situation. He'd call when they got in, see if Sybil could have a drink with them. Then he'd casually work the conversation around to Amour Graphics. See what developed.

Jan accepted a plastic cup filled with ice cubes and very little cola from the stewardess, giving the woman a friendly but distant smile. She was still tired. The catnap at L'Amour had only made it more difficult to fall asleep when she'd driven home.

Doug had followed her, making sure that she didn't fall asleep en route. Jan was relieved when he didn't ask to come in. He had kissed her good night and gone home. She hadn't seen him again until he'd picked her up for the trip to the airport.

Why had he helped her? Was it all part of the plot he and Jason had cooked up?

She wanted to believe it. And yet she didn't.

The mental battle had kept her sleepless when she was dropping with fatigue.

"Still tired?" Doug asked.

Jan sighed. "Guess so."

"Poor darling. Let's put the chair arm up and

223

I'll act as your pillow while you take a nap."

Cuddled in his arms, her head resting against his chest, Jan listened to the steady beat of his heart and wondered if Doug would love her if she were indeed poor.

Probably not.

Chapter Thirteen

It was while she dozed that the doubt began to grow.

Ever since the going-away party, she had been laboring under the belief that Clifford had been right, that Doug was merely after her money.

But what if Cliff had gotten it all wrong?

In which case, she was maligning Doug in believing he was a fortune hunter. He'd been extremely helpful, volunteering for duty in the kitchen, and again at L'Amour the night before. She hadn't asked either time. He'd just pitched in. And he'd taken over the delivery chores for her that morning so that she could sleep in.

More importantly, when she'd left the opening for him to jump in with a repeated suggestion that she sell the graphics shop, he had let it pass without a comment.

The look in his eyes was tender, not avaricious. And the feel of his cheek resting against her hair as she drowsed was very pleasant.

Yet it all came down to one indisputable fact. Even if he really was only interested in Simon

Ingraham's estate, she still loved him. As long as Doug didn't do anything to prove Cliff's tale true, she was going to keep on loving him and hope he grew to love her.

The decision brought Jan peace. She settled more comfortably in Doug's arms, and drifted off to sleep.

Jan slept nearly the whole flight, rousing only when Doug told her it was time to buckle her seat belt. The nap had revived her, put the sparkle back in her eyes. The mental struggle was behind her, and the once longed-for hours with Doug lay ahead.

As she blinked sleep from her eyes, Doug grinned lazily at her. He looked so handsome with his hair falling in glossy, natural waves and that special light glowing in his slate gray eyes. She'd been distracted with weariness when they'd worked their way through the air terminal in Ohio, but she'd still noticed the way women's eyes followed him. And he'd had eyes only for her.

Her fortune. Her. What difference did it make? At least for the time they were in San Francisco, Jan swore she wouldn't let such thoughts cross her mind. Doug had invited her on this weekend trip because he cared. She wouldn't inquire too deeply into what it was he cared for. She would just enjoy their days together. Enjoy them thoroughly.

San Francisco was a very romantic city. When the plane landed, the sun was retreating, leaving the sky to the moon and the stars. To lovers.

Doug splurged, bypassing the airport buses into the city in favor of a taxi. Rather than look at the sights, Jan preferred to continue snuggling in Doug's arms. Would she ever know if it was love that radiated from his eyes? She'd known lust before, but never love.

Their room at the Hyatt Regency had a lovely view — if you ignored the office building on the right and stared out over the Embarcadero Freeway to the inner bay. Gray and mauve sectionals created an L-shaped living area. Behind it the wall was mirrored. A welcoming arrangement of fresh flowers was placed in the center of a glass coffee table. Two upholstered chairs bracketed the conversation area, turning their backs on the long window and a portable bar. A screen was folded back to display the queen-sized bed. Jan was amused to find the bed was angled so that it not only faced a television, but allowed the occupants to admire themselves in the full-length mirrored closet doors.

Jan glanced from the bed to the mirror to Doug. He raised and lowered his eyebrows in a comic leer. Jan dissolved into giggles.

"Come here," he said quietly.

"Oh, I can't," she gasped, still laughing. "Not now."

Doug closed the space between them. His arm

went around her, lifted her off her feet. Together they fell onto the bed. With her sprawled beneath him on the mattress, Doug glanced over at their reflection in the mirror.

Jan's giggles increased. The merry sound filled the room with joy, filled his heart with love. Ignoring the mirror, Doug smoothed back her curls, cupped Jan's face in his hands. "I don't know how I did it," he murmured smiling down into her eyes.

His tender expression stilled her mirth. She savored the feel of his fingertips in her hair, the hard length of his body covering hers. "Did what?" she asked a bit breathless.

"Stayed away from you," he answered quietly.

"You were busy."

"You haunted me," he said. "I couldn't eat. Couldn't sleep. I was miserable."

Her eyes were wide, her mouth parted in awe. "You too?"

Oh, it was so easy to forget her misgivings about him, so easy to give in to the need to fall in love with him.

"I didn't trust myself to talk to you," he whispered. His lips dropped to lightly caress hers, then moved on to taste the tip of her nose, her eyelids.

"I missed you so dreadfully," Jan said.

"You're so beautiful."

"No, I'm not. I'm—"

His mouth stopped the words. This time he

wasn't tender. There was an urgency in his kiss, a need so primeval that he was unable to suppress it any longer. It was punishingly sweet, his lips slanting hungrily over hers, the force pressing her deeper into the pillows.

The thread of sanity snapped within Jan as well. With a throaty sigh, she responded, losing her hands in his thick hair. Her lips parted, her tongue met his in the age-old dance of shared passion.

Doug's hands skimmed down her body, pulling Jan closer against him. "God, I want you." His voice was harsh with longing. "But if we don't change, we'll be late."

"Late," Jan repeated, still a bit dazed.

"We have reservations for the show at the Fairmont."

"Oh, of course." She eased from his arms. Shrugged off the white jacket, letting it drop to the floor.

Doug didn't move from his reclining position on the bed. He gazed at the way her bare shoulders gleamed in the light, how the closet door mirror allowed him a glimpse of the low dipping back of her dress.

Jan reached behind her and slowly slid the zipper down. She unfastened the button at the nape of her neck. The dress dropped to her hips. "Couldn't we be late?" she asked.

His eyes followed each of her movements, lingered on each newly exposed inch of sun touched ivory skin. Languidly his glance moved up to her lovely, blushing face. Doug sat up and grinned. The roguish smirk Jan associated with Stark Savage. The smile that made her heart act strangely.

"Sugar," Doug purred huskily, holding out his hand to her in an invitation, "we don't even have to go."

They did reach the Fairmont. Late. Very late. Jan had no idea who they'd come to see. But the jazz combo, with the tinkling piano, lazy trombone, throbbing bass, and hushed brush of the drums, suited her mellow mood to a T.

They had dressed separately, knowing that close proximity would only lead them back to the bed. Jan had taken over the bathroom. When she emerged it was with a horrible feeling of self-doubt. She hadn't been interested in attending her high school prom, hadn't belonged to a sorority in college. There had never been an occasion for her to wear, much less own, a gown like the scarlet cocktail dress Charlotte had chosen for her. With its dipping neckline, dropped shoulder sleeves, and puffy tiers of wide ruffled skirt, the red dress was a fairytale gown.

She felt like Cinderella poised at the top of the stairs at the ball, wondering why she was there, and if Prince Charming was worth it.

Doug looked like a stranger and incredibly

handsome in his dark blue suit, pale striped shirt, and patterned necktie.

Jan stood hesitating, her hands gripped together.

His eyes skimmed over her, lingering on her exposed shoulders. She'd worn the gold necklace but no other accessories. Her dark brown curls clustered around her ears. She'd used a hint of eye shadow, and a touch of lipstick. And was extremely self-conscious about both.

Doug gulped. Cleared his throat. "God, but you're lovely, Janelle Ingraham," he mumbled huskily.

The dress was a definite hit. At the Fairmont, the combo dropped into a sensuous version of the old Errol Gardner favorite, *Misty*. Seated at a small table in the dark with Doug's arm draped possessively over the back of her chair, Jan listened to the smoky-voiced singer. She felt the words of the song fit the way she was feeling. She was indeed as helpless as a kitten up a tree. She still tingled from the delightfully hasty joining in the hotel. Christening their room, Doug had called it, his grin positively sardonic. Lord, but she loved the way he smiled.

And looked, and felt, and smelled, and tasted, and moved, and . . .

Jan sighed. And made love. That wasn't all though. She respected his work, admired the way he had pulled three absolutely wonderful letterhead ideas out of the blue, the way he'd convinced Charlotte Penn that her concept of the sales brochures was all wrong. The way he pitched in, no matter what the project, from collecting vines to delivering artwork.

She'd been fascinated by him ever since that first kiss. No, longer. Since she'd found him lounging in the doorway at L'Amour, those broad shoulders propped against the molding, an amused smirk on his lips.

And now he was all hers. At least for this single weekend.

They drank white wine and gazed into each other's eyes. The combo finished their set, but Jan and Doug lingered, one of the last couples to leave the showroom. From the Fairmont, Doug took her across to the Mark Hopkins Hotel, and up the elevator to the rooftop bar. They had a leisurely drink, neither particularly thirsty for anything but each other. Gazing into each other's eyes was preferable to admiring the awe-inspiring 360-degree view from the Top of the Mark. By two in the morning when the bars closed their liquor cabinets, Jan and Doug were back in their room, conscious only of each other.

He moved the screen so that it blocked the closet door mirror. But he also opened the vertical blinds at the window so that the view from the bed was of stars.

Doug woke once during the night, conscious that Jan was no longer at his side. She was a wraith at the window, a wispy peach silk robe wrapped around her lithe form.

Doug raised himself, leaning back on his elbows. "Jan?"

She turned slightly, floated back to his side. The silk whispered with her movement. Parted over her long, lovely legs when she curled up on the bed again. "The fog has rolled in," she said.

Earlier, the view had drawn her with its myriad dancing lights on the bay, the running lights of moored vessels. It had been a magical world so achingly beautiful it had made Jan's breath catch.

They'd stood before the window gazing out at the fairyland, her back pressed against his chest, his arms linked lightly beneath her breasts. "Thank you for bringing me here," Jan had whispered.

Now the same breathless tone was in her voice.

"The fog?" Doug echoed.

Jan nodded, turned back to look out the window at the enveloping white mantle.

Doug touched her chin, turned her face back to press a feathery kiss on her lips. "How would you like to go walking in the fog with me, beautiful?"

Somewhere to the east the sun was rising over the hills out in the Walnut Creek and Danville

233

areas, already burning off the mist. But in the city, the cloak kept the streets shrouded in mystery.

Dressed in sweaters, jeans, and high tops, Doug and Jan ambled through the hush of early Saturday morning. They walked the length of Justin Herman Plaza situated at the rear of the hotel. Devoid of the street performers, skateboarders, and the bustle of the day, it belonged to lovers. Doug's arm lay around Jan's shoulders, hers around his waist, her head on his shoulder. They didn't talk, just strolled, each content with these quietly shared moments. Up the narrow width of Clay, past the linked blocks of the Embarcadero Center shopping mall, to Kearny then north. With Portsmouth Square, now a part of Chinatown, on their left, they continued down past the tall pinnacle of the Transatlantic Pyramid and turned right to wander through the streets of Jackson Square. The century-old buildings housed the shops of designers and decorators, even a shop that specialized in maps of the world, and of all ages.

The mist tightened the curl of Jan's hair, gave it a damp sheen. Her lashes glittered with moisture, her cheeks and eyes glowed with pleasure. When they returned to the Hyatt Regency she shivered a bit beneath Doug's arm. He hustled her to the elevator, kissed her as it mounted swiftly through the still-sleeping hotel to their floor. Once inside their room, Doug insisted on warming her in a hot shower—shared—then to ensure that the chill of the mist was gone, took Jan back to bed.

Her eager response to each successive step convinced him that she was extremely healthy.

And he fell still further in love with her.

Doug sat across from Jan in the coffee shop sipping a cup of coffee. He was amazed at the amount of food she'd just polished off. "That is the most food I've ever seen you put away," he mused lolling back in his chair.

Jan gave him a dazzling, mischievous smile. "Excessive exercise makes me ravenous."

"Excessive?"

"Let me rephrase that," Jan said, licking a dab of jelly from her fingertip. "Call it delightful. I wouldn't want you to think I wasn't appreciative."

He grinned back at her, lazily content with life. After all, Jan had appeared very appreciative—and eager. "Delightful will suffice," Doug allowed. "And since I have every intention of continuing the delightful exercise, perhaps we ought to keep an eye peeled for an all-you-can-eat smorgasbord today."

Jan blushed.

It was very satisfying for Doug's ego.

They discussed sights to visit, deciding to forgo Alcatraz in favor of a ferry trip to Sausalito, skipping the larger museums to cruise the shops at Ghirardelli Square, the Cannery, and Pier 39. When Ghirardelli's ice cream was mentioned, Jan hastened to remind Doug that he still owed her a hot fudge sundae. Doug vetoed guided tours, insisting that they could hit the high spots faster on their own. In quick succession he listed Coit Tower, the Golden Gate Bridge, and Nob Hill. They'd been up the hill the evening before, but riding one of the famous trolley cars up it was a treat not to be missed. However, there were two museums Doug insisted be on their list. One was next door to the Maritime Museum—the floating section of the exhibits, the ships riding at anchor at the Hyde Street Pier. The other museum was open only on Wednesday and Sunday afternoons. Built in the 1880s, the Haas-Lilienthal House on Franklin Street was contemporary with the farmhouse Jan rented, but the architectural details and original family furnishings were a treat no one should miss, Doug claimed.

Jan finished her breakfast, revitalized for the day. Doug watched her, the energetic way she moved, nearly bouncing with excitement. A thousand other breakfasts together stretched before them. He savored the thought of each one.

Doug stood up, held out his hand. "San Francisco awaits, sugar."

Jan slid her hand in his. Their fingers entwined. What was it about him, she wondered, that made it so easy to negate her fears, to trust him? To love him. And within such a short span of time to know she'd never feel this special with anyone else.

Together, they left the hotel. At the junction of California and Drumm streets a few early visitors huffed their way up from the underground BART station, the efficient mass transit system. It was an older mode of travel that drew Jan. While Doug purchased all-day trolley tickets from a machine, she gazed in awe at the cable car that sat patiently on its rails, only a few feet away.

Tall structures of steel, glass, and concrete rose around them, reaching toward a now cloudless sky. Ahead lay the financial district, and the impossibly steep climb up California Street.

"Come on." Taking her hand again, Doug urged Jan into a half run to the waiting trolley. Jan had barely settled into one of the outer seats, with Doug towering over her, his arm wrapped around a pole, his feet wedged between hers, when the conductor rang his bell. The cable car jerked into motion with a loud grinding of gears.

Jan stared around at everything the noisy vehicle passed, wide-eyed at the Wells Fargo Bank and its neighbors, at the glimpse of Chinatown as the car chugged across Grant and Stockton streets. Bay-windowed buildings passed, automobiles darted around the slower-moving trolley, taking the climb at a steady clip.

Doug admired only the glowing woman before him. Excitement nearly bubbled from Jan when the conductor clanged the bell before crossing each intersection. She was breathless looking down the steep slope of California Street and marveled naively that anyone could walk up it, or that the cable could support the weight of the loaded car.

People got off, others hopped on. Jan's eyes grew wider trying to cover everything, to miss nothing. Doug grew even more enchanted with her.

They got off at the crest of the hill to stroll around the hotels and tightly packed townhomes. At the foot of Nob Hill lay one of the oldest American parts of the town. It had been the area where the Gold Rush miners had first stumbled off ships believing nuggets lay like gravel on the streets. Portsmouth Square had hummed with activity then. Saloons, gambling halls, and bordellos had been among the earliest businesses. Mercantile companies, freighters, stagecoach lines, shipping lines, barbers, bakers, and bankers had followed on their heels. Constructed mainly of canvas and timber, the town had burned to the ground frequently in the early years. A lot had changed since then. Not only had the building materials become more durable, the way people spoke of the city had altered. Back in the mining era it had answered to the fond nickname of "Frisco." Now "Frisco," residents were at pains to explain, was a trolley car. They lived in *San Francisco*.

The city had had its roots shaken and buildings destroyed, the result of earthquakes in 1906 and 1989. Levi Strauss had made his fortune constructing hard-wearing denim trousers in San Francisco. The Bank of America's birth belonged to the city. Tony Bennett claimed to have left his heart there.

Doug's first visit to the City by the Bay had been on a job interview. He hadn't taken the position because it hadn't offered any new vistas for him. But it was how he'd met Sybil Adler. He hoped she hadn't changed her mind since they'd last talked. He was banking his future on Sybil's answer when they met her for a drink later.

That was hours away and Jan was glowing as they strolled hand in hand through the city.

The Big Four, the Railroad Barons who pushed the tracks eastward to meet the Union Pacific in the wilds of Utah, had made Nob Hill the home of the millionaires over a century ago. Most of their mansions were gone now, only the names remained, honored by places like the Mark Hopkins Hotel which stood at 1 Nob Hill, the site of Hopkins's home.

One weekend wasn't enough to allow for leisurely walks through the city and hit the high points on a tourist's itinerary. Tugging at her hand, Doug pulled Jan after him, back to catch the Powell Street trolley down a different angle of the hill, bound for the pier. She squealed delightfully and clutched his arm when the cable car began its sharp descent. It made Doug feel like he'd brought her to a carnival. It was a wonderful feeling.

The day went by far too quickly. The wind off the bay whipped at them on the pier as they clambered through the old ferryboat and a tall-masted sailing ship. Jan voiced a preference for the wooden vessel and lingered in the hold gazing at the rough-hewn timbers, then in the companionway to soak up the atmosphere in the captain's cabin.

Doug wanted to savor these moments watching Jan lost in thought, her eyes gleaming, her lips soft and parted, her cheeks glowing. She turned with a quick smile and Doug's heart expanded. God, he loved her.

Surprisingly enough, when they visited the shops, Jan collected business cards rather than merchandise. The businesses didn't all specialize in her type of crafts, but he felt sure she knew other artists and artisans who would benefit from her thoughtfulness.

When she shivered in the cool breeze off the bay, Doug bought her a sweatshirt at one of the many streetside vendors. It was pink with baby blue lettering that announced she'd visited San Francisco. A souvenir, he insisted when Jan protested. Her curls were even more tousled when he pulled it over her head. The blue of her eyes was heightened by the color of the fleecy shirt. He spent the rest of the day planning to peel the garment off her.

Sybil had suggested she meet them at the San Francisco Brewery, a cozy little bar on Columbus. Only Sybil had called it by its original name, The Albatross. The bar was one of the oldest in town, having begun life as a waterfront dive complete with trapdoor for the removal of shanghaied sailors. That had been back in time though, and now the waterfront was a good bit further away, filled in years ago by residents impatient with the geologic time scale and eager for land expansion.

"The way you carry on about historic houses, you'll love the joint," Sybil had said when Doug had called earlier. "Antique bar, tiled trough spittoon around it for tobacco chewers — not used currently, I'm thankful to say — and the quaintest fan system you'll ever see."

It was an echo of the miners' Frisco. The older, other side of a city that seemed mostly glass and concrete around the Embarcadero, and all hills and bow-front windows elsewhere.

Doug and Jan had little time to admire the place, or the faded wooden "Albatross" sign tucked away nearly out of sight above the door inside. They took a quick gander at the antique pulley system that rotated equally antique-look-

241

ing palm fans to stir the air in the room. The clientele had changed greatly from the Gold Rush days. It appeared to be strictly up-and-coming young urbanites. They passed an intense couple discussing their chances of being chosen for a part in an approaching theatrical production. Another couple, both of the same sex, were busily tearing apart a local exhibition of paintings.

Sybil waved from a table in the back, urging them to hurry.

Jan had been leery of meeting the unknown woman. Although Doug had said she wasn't an old flame, it wasn't until Jan actually saw Sybil Adler pump his hand rather than embrace Doug that she relaxed. Doug introduced the two women and asked what everyone was drinking. While he went to the bar to place their order, Sybil settled in her chair and asked Jan what she thought of San Francisco.

Sybil was a good bit older than either of them, Jan realized. She wore her dark hair in a skull-hugging cap and seemed to be cultivating, rather than hiding, distinguished-looking gray streaks back from her temples. She was mannish in build and in mannerisms. Far from a fashion plate, Sybil wore loose tweed trousers, a dark turtleneck pullover, tailored suit jacket and sensible low-heeled oxfords. On her left hand she wore a wide wedding ring. Jan wondered if Sybil belonged to the gay community, but when Doug returned with three mugs of beer, that idea was killed aborning.

"How are Peter and the kids?" he asked.

Sybil savored her beer. "Pains in the ass, all three of them." She glanced over at Jan. "My husband's decided to have a mid-life crisis just when I'm ready to wring the kids' necks for being teenaged jerks. Thank God I can get away from them all at work."

"Sybil's a member of the Institute of Graphic Designers here in San Francisco," Doug explained. "She interviewed me for a job a few years back and is still mad that I turned her down."

The woman frowned, took another gulp of beer. "You're good, but not irreplaceable, MacLeod."

She looked over at Jan. "I understand you're in the biz, too. You familiar with the work of the Institute? We've got some extremely talented members, and they deal with a wide variety of projects. Exhibition design, architectural signing, modular signing, merchandising systems, master planning. All the mediums, too. Photography, illustration, production from start to finish. Members deal with big clients, places like CBS, Paramount, Wells Fargo, Corning, AT&T. You get the picture. Pressure stuff."

Jan wondered what Sybil Adler was warming up to. How it involved her. For it most definitely did. Doug was leaning back in his chair rather detached from the conversation now. And Sybil was focusing on Jan.

"I've been in it all since '66," Sybil said. "I skipped the protests at Berkeley and apprenticed with firms like Harry Murphy + Friends and Robert Pease & Company when they first came to San Francisco. Met my husband at the same time. He's a photographer. Now it's time to move out on our own."

Jan began to get a bad feeling.

"Trouble is, I'm sick of the city. The pace is too wearing. Peter doesn't give a fig one way or another, but I want someplace fresh, yet near enough to the metropolis to edge in on the business there."

It was coming, Jan thought. She glanced at Doug. He was still relaxed, almost removed from the proceedings. Despite all the tender loving, the romantic evening, the whirlwind day of sightseeing and shopping, he had set her up.

"MacLeod here tells me you've got a graphics company in Indiana you're interested in unloading." Sybil Adler said. "I've been investigating some other options, like starting from scratch, but I'd like to hear about your place."

Jan's hands tightened around her barely touched mug of beer. She didn't feel the moisture condensing along its sides, or the beveled design of the glass. The only thing she felt was betrayed.

Chapter Fourteen

Jan had no memory of leaving the bar. She had a vague impression that she hadn't embarrassed herself, or Doug, in front of Sybil Adler. She'd babbled something about only just acquiring Amour Graphics and still investigating different avenues, one being the possible sale. She didn't commit herself to anything, not even to letting the Adler woman know if she did decide to sell.

It wasn't until they were back in their room at the Hyatt Regency that Jan blew up.

"What right did you have to tell anyone Amour was for sale?" she stormed, struggling out of the sweatshirt Doug had bought her. She flung it aside on the sectional, grabbed her suitcase and dumped it down on the bed. Then she headed for the closet.

Doug cut her off, his hands on her shoulders. "Didn't you tell me just yesterday that . . ."

Jan shrugged him off. "Clifford was right, wasn't he? I was willing to give you the benefit

245

of the doubt, but good old drunken Cliff hit the nail right on the head."

"What are you talking about?" Doug's voice had risen in volume, but there was only puzzlement in his tone.

Jan stripped her clothes off the hangers, the red dress, the sundress she'd traveled in, the outfit she'd planned to dazzle him with later that evening. "The plot you and Jason cooked up. The one where everyone gets an heiress."

A slow burning flush worked up Doug's neck. "Cliff told you that?"

Jan watched as his face turned red. With fury for being found out?

"Hell!" Doug spat. "And you believed him?"

"He's my friend. Was he lying?"

She was far too calm now. He had preferred her anger. Now, whatever he said, it was going to hurt her.

"Yes. And no. But it isn't like you think, Jan."

"It never is," she said, opened her suitcase and began folding her clothes inside.

"I was protecting you."

"Really?" The calm was turning to frost.

"Jan," Doug said, trying again. He touched her shoulder.

"Please don't touch me."

His hand dropped away. "I love you," he said.

"Be honest, Doug. It's Uncle Simon's money you really care about." Jan snapped the suitcase closed, slung her oversized purse over her shoulder, and hefted the bag off the bed. "Thank you for a very pleasant trip. Last night and the sightseeing earlier were very special. However, I believe it would be best if you didn't try to contact me again, Doug."

Turning her back on him, Jan marched to the door, and out of his life.

Jan was proud of herself. She didn't cry in the elevator to the lobby. She remained calm and collected during the airport taxi ride. She even managed to look like she was reading the slick formatted airline magazine when she was seated on a plane bound for home. No one else knew that she turned the pages without seeing a single word.

She'd been lucky to find a flight, much less a seat. There had been less than an hour's wait till departure. Jan had used the time to call her parents. Although she would change planes twice with long layovers en route, her final destination would be Indianapolis. She didn't want to go back to Richmond. Not now. Maybe never.

"Sweetheart!" was her mother's greeting when Jan arrived at Weir Cook Municipal Airport early the next morning. "You look terrible."

"Who wouldn't, being awake all night?" Jan hugged her.

"I'm not talking about that, dear. This is worse than sleeplessness. What's his name?"

So Jan cried all the way back to her parents'

house, and part of the next day as well. Her father called Jason Holloway and asked him to open Amour Graphics long enough to change the message on the answering machine and hang a sign on the door that it was closed due to illness.

By the end of the week Jan felt calm enough to return to her farmhouse in Richmond, to pick up her new life as sole employee of Amour Graphics. She avoided seeing her old friends and wished there had been some way to duck Charlotte Penn. The last proved impossible though.

Charlotte was lying in wait for her at the office. Perched on the desktop, her legs swinging, her wispy tea skirt floating with each motion, Charlotte was busily trying to talk Mrs. Fine's ear off.

Jan had noticed that while Charlotte advocated business suits for her, Charlotte herself never appeared in such tailored apparel. She preferred to play the ethereal fairy godmother flitting about in gauzy dresses that seemed more suited to luncheon on the White House lawn.

"Dear Jan!" Charlotte cooed. "At last I've caught you. When you didn't answer the RSVP on your invitation for my little housewarming I feared the worst! You look quite pale. Still suffering from that dastardly flu bug Jason told me you'd caught?"

Flu, Jan thought. So that's what her father had invented to explain her absence. Couldn't he have thought of something more long-term or contagious? Something like smallpox that would have kept people like Charlotte away.

"I realized, of course," Charlotte babbled on, "that you received the invitation when you were ill and obviously responding skipped your mind. So I've just come by to remind you that it's tomorrow night. Around eight. Wear that delightful red gown we found for you. No presents necessary, just your lovely presence.

"I am quite eager to show the place off. Jason's paintings make the house come alive, I must tell you. By this time next year, he'll be quite the rage."

Jan let Charlotte babble on. She really didn't need to hear how Charlotte's life was all sweetness and light since Jason had entered it. It seemed that while her own life crumbled around her, everyone else's perked up. Even Aunt Beatrice had announced her intention of marrying Walter, the lawyer. Meanwhile, things at Amour Graphics disintegrated more each day. Accounts that had been with Lloyd for years, now found the quotes from other companies more attractive.

Who could blame them? Jan admitted. She was only one person. She couldn't be sales rep, illustrator, copysetter, and graphics layout artist all in one. It wasn't just the time restraints. She didn't want to be even one of those things, much less all of them.

Probate had finished on Simon's will. She'd turned over the agreed-upon amount to Lloyd and Sandy's bank. She placed another ten thousand in the graphics account to cover expenses, such as rent and the temporary agency fee for Mrs. Fine's continued assistance. The accountant warned her that the income was all gone from the accounts Doug had helped her finish the work on. By the end of summer he'd have to dip into her personal funds again.

Worst of all, it had been nearly two months since she'd had time to work on her crafts. A month since she'd seen Jason, Clifford, or Angie.

She tried not to count the days since she'd walked out of the hotel in San Francisco, leaving Doug behind.

"I brought you another map so you'll have no trouble finding the house," Charlotte bubbled, beaming equally at Mrs. Fine and Jan. She slid off the desk. Her skirt settled around her legs, dropping nearly to her ankles. "I must fly now, dear Jan. Do be on time. There are some people I want you to meet."

Jan groaned to herself and went into the back room. She still had work to do on projects for the few accounts Amour Graphics still held.

She no longer thought of the business as L'Amour.

Charlotte's house was a mock-Tudor set back from the road amid a copse of mature red oak. While mulberry accented the long stretch of

250

lawn. Rosebushes decorated the flowerbeds near the main double doors and colored an arbored garden at one corner of the property.

Only the gates at either end of the long horseshoe-shaped drive were visible from the road. Jan found the party by following the procession of expensive cars that cruised through the entrance gate.

She felt strange coming alone. But she had no intention of calling Clifford to see if he was going. He wanted to live in Charlotte's pocket, had failed her when she needed him at Amour. Had been the one to suggest Doug was perfidious.

Clifford was no longer counted among her friends.

Neither, of course, were any of the freelancers. She had felt shunned by them even before they'd all ducked out on her. She had fulfilled the dreams they'd all talked about. Had bought Lloyd out. And they had turned on her.

Well, so be it. She didn't need them. Once she decided what she wanted to do, maybe she'd just leave the area. The only thing that was holding her in Richmond was Amour Graphics.

Jan pulled her Oldsmobile in behind a shiny black Rolls-Royce, followed its example and cruised up to the entrance where a uniformed valet attendant jumped to open her door. Trying to act as if such service was an everyday occurrence, Jan stepped out, her red dress rustling. She wobbled a bit on her spiked heels. The valet steadied her with a hand on her elbow. His eyes swept down her, taking in the sequin bows on her shoes, continuing up over black stockings and on to her bare shoulders. Her gold necklace encircled her throat, gold dangled at her ears. Blusher colored her cheeks, shadow enhanced her eyes. Her curls were tamed and arranged with the help of a ton of mousse. Where once she'd felt beautiful in the dress, Jan now felt she should be leaning against a lamppost. She shouldn't have come to Charlotte's party.

"Easy there," the valet said. He probably wasn't more than eighteen, Jan thought.

"Thank you," she mumbled.

"No problem." Jan could almost hear him mentally add "baby" to the phrase. He handed her a claim ticket, slid behind the wheel, and moved her car into the woods, angling it off the drive.

Jan squared her shoulders and approached the door.

It stood wide open framing an exquisitely gowned Charlotte Penn. Her blond hair was up-swept and adorned with diamond clips. Diamonds sparkled on her shoulder in the pin that appeared to be all that clasped the bodice of her Grecian draped gown together. It was wispy-looking, as all of Charlotte's clothing seemed to be, but this time the antique ivory color did nasty things to Charlotte's complexion. The gown matched the one in the large painting on the wall behind her though. Obviously Charlotte was playing at having stepped from the canvas.

Jan was swept into a suffocating embrace, overwhelmed with the sweet cloying essence of Charlotte's perfume. Charlotte touched cheeks with Jan and passed her on to an older man with faded blond hair who was hastily introduced as Charles Penn, Charlotte's father. The elder Penn pushed Jan farther into the house and turned to greet the next guest.

Would they really have missed her if she hadn't come?

Jan wandered through the rooms, staring at paintings she'd been familiar with for years. There was probably even one of her somewhere, although she doubted anyone would recognize her as the subject. Jason had been attempting an impressionistic style and set up his easel in her front yard. While she'd picked over her harvest of wildflowers, he'd tried for genius. Although in Jan's estimation, he had more than achieved it, Jason hadn't been overly fond of his creation. He never was though. A perfectionist, Jason had never been able to see the verve and magnetism of his own brush.

It was in the room with the bar that she found the originals of the romance covers displayed. Jan tried to avoid them, uneasy about seeing the painting of her and Doug as Aphrodite and Stark. She was just turning away when someone seized her arm.

"Jannie!" a familiar voice crooned. "Is that really you?"

Jan plastered a smile on her face. "Hello,

Cliff. No, I don't think it is me. How's the screenplay coming?"

"Fine, fine." He had a tumbler in his hand. Kentucky bourbon—neat by the smell of it and Cliff's breath. At any rate, it was a change from bubblegum. "So what do you think of all this?" He waved a hand recklessly.

"Interesting," Jan replied. "I haven't seen much. I just got here."

"Ah, then let me show you around." Cliff turned Jan back to the illustrations for the book covers. "You never saw the last one, did you? *Passion's Final Frontier.*"

She didn't particularly want to now.

Cliff wasn't taking no for an answer. Jan lifted her chin, prayed for courage, and turned toward the wall.

It was worse than she had expected.

Although she and Doug had not posed for this cover, Jason had taken a bit of artistic license and superimposed their faces on those of his models. In a way it made sense, Jan supposed. There was continuity between the characters pictured on both of the *Passion* books.

On this one, Stark Savage was on his back. Aphrodite Cartwright was posed above him, straddling his torso. Her skirts were hitched up, her long blond hair tossed over her shoulder, away from the viewer. The bodice of her dress was just opening, allowing a good deal of her breast to flow toward Stark's waiting hand.

The worst part was the expression on Aphro-

dite's face. Her face, Jan thought. That was ec-
stasy if she'd ever seen it. Unfortunately she had.
Reflected in her own cheval glass and in the mirror at the Hyatt Regency.

"Great, isn't it?" Cliff said.

"I like some of Jase's other stuff better," Jan
said.

"Well, show me which one. First we need to
get you a drink."

Jan asked the bartender for a Virgin Mary.
She still had to drive home. Once she got there
then she'd drink to try and forget this evening.

To avoid Cliff's drunken camaraderie earlier,
Doug had hastened up the circular staircase in
the library. It had put him face to face with
what he considered Jason's least inspired work.
In his opinion, Holloway's style didn't adapt to
the impressionistic school. But then he'd been
privy to Jason's genius from the beginning. He
was probably a tougher audience than some —
and that had a lot to do with downright envy
for Holloway's talent.

Doug strode along the upper gallery heading
for the hall. One painting caught his attention.
It wasn't the excitement present in every brush
stroke that halted his steps. It was the subject.

Jan.

He knew it was her. Not just because the
farmhouse behind her was recognizable. It was
the way the indistinct figure held herself. The

way her head tilted. The way her dark curls appeared to dance in the breeze. The girl in the painting was turned away, her profile hazy. She held a collection of long-stemmed wildflowers in her arms, as gently as if they were a baby. In fact, if you didn't know who it was, and where the picture had been painted, the blurred bundle that she cradled could have been a child.

Jan.

He still couldn't get the memory of her ice-edged fury out of his mind.

After she'd sailed out of their room in San Francisco, he'd wished her to the devil. Had told himself he was relieved that she'd left him. She'd saved him from making a bigger fool of himself by asking her to marry him.

So what had he done? He'd gone down to the bar and sunk deeper into misery. Despite one hell of a hangover, he'd visited every spot they'd planned to see. And late Sunday night, he'd caught the plane back home, terribly conscious of the empty seat next to him.

Had she come to Charlotte's *little party?*

Doug forced himself to continue out of the room, to find a back staircase and get the hell out of the house. He felt claustrophobic surrounded by Jason's paintings. It had been bad enough at Holloway's house. But at least most of them had been turned to the wall there.

Doug didn't find an escape route until he had visited every room on the upper level. He'd rejected the main staircase immediately. He would be more likely to run into Charlotte, or Cliff, or worse—Jan. There was only one reason he'd accepted the invitation. That was to confront Jason.

The master suite was a series of rooms. A sitting room, dressing room with adjacent bath (with Roman tub), and the bedroom itself. Jason's paintings hung on every wall in every room.

Off the sitting room was a wide wooden deck with a staircase leading down to the pool in back. A good number of guests had drifted around it.

He made his way down the steps, and nearly bumped into Jason coming up them.

"MacLeod!" Jason cried with pleasure. "How long have you been here?"

"Long enough," Doug snarled. "A real change seeing all your work facing front, isn't it?"

Jason always turned his canvases against the wall in his own house.

Holloway laughed. "Lotty's idea, buddy, not mine. How have you been?"

He'd been lousy ever since Jan had left him standing in their room in San Francisco. "Can I talk to you somewhere, Jase? Privately?"

Holloway looked surprised, then waved his arm, directing Doug toward the side of the house.

Like Doug, Jason was dressed in a tuxedo. The difference being Holloway's had probably been custom-made and his was off the rack,

Doug thought. Jason's face wasn't looking quite so gaunt anymore either. Life with Charlotte agreed with him.

Jason led the way to a secluded patio. Wide windows were open in the adjacent room, but it was dark inside. The din of the crowd appeared a bit muted as well.

The curtains stirred in the evening breeze. Inside the house the temperature had dropped to the low seventies, thanks to the hard-working air conditioning system. Some cold soul had probably opened the windows to warm the place up.

It was a very pleasant evening outside. And the secluded patio fit Doug's plans perfectly.

"Here we are," Jason announced and turned back to face Doug. "Now what did you—"

Doug's fist hit him square in the mouth.

Jason went down like a sapling under the ax. He lay sprawled on his back, his expression stunned. "What was that for?" Jason demanded, touching his lip tenderly. Blood came away on his fingers.

"For thinking I'm just as mercenary as you. Thanks a lot, pal," Doug snarled. "You lost me the only woman I care about."

Jason blinked up at him. "Jannie?"

"Hell, yes, Jan. You told Clifford I was after her money, you son-of-a-bitch."

"And you aren't?" Holloway sounded amazed at the news. He touched his lip again.

"Damn it, Jase. Get up so I can knock you down again. I don't care about Jan's money. For

258

all I care she can buy a hundred graphics companies or donate the whole thing to the bloody Society for the Prevention of Cruelty to Lunchbags."

Jason held up both hands. "Okay, okay. I'm sorry. I didn't know." He rolled over on one knee, pushing himself up. "You really love her?" His voice still sounded stunned at the news.

Impatient, Doug reached down to drag his former roommate back on his feet.

"Damn it," Jason groaned. "I didn't know."

"That's because you're a total ass, Holloway," Doug growled. He took a deep breath, his hands still clenched in fists.

"Feel better now?" Jason asked. "Or do you want me to lie down and bleed some more?"

Chapter Fifteen

Jan stayed back in the shadows, her presence hidden by the billowing curtains.

She'd never seen a man strike another outside of the movies and television. And that was all fake. But it wasn't fake blood that trickled down from the corner of Jason's mouth.

She should be shocked, Jan supposed. She should be appalled. She should not be this happy about seeing Doug plant his fist square on Jason's kisser.

But she did. She felt gloriously happy.

When the two men moved back toward the guests around the pool, Jason with Doug's folded handkerchief pressed to his lip, Jan retraced her steps out of the room.

She'd been escaping Charlotte herself when she'd found the deserted corridor. It had been bad enough having Cliff drag her around the entire exhibit of paintings. Charlotte's good intentions on top of that were more than any woman could endure in one evening. Jan had planned to sneak out of the house, back around the side, present her valet ticket, and get the hell out of there.

She hadn't expected to have her world turned upside down.

Again.

He hadn't been lying! Her heart did strange flip-flops, as if it were doing cartwheels. It was really true! Doug didn't have any interest in her inheritance.

And, best of all, he loved her!

He'd told her and she hadn't believed him. He'd asked her to marry him the afternoon of the picnic. She hadn't believed him then either.

Dear God! Doug had been saying everything she wanted to hear and she'd been deaf!

Jan worked her way back to the crowded main rooms of the house and, in a real change of face, sought Charlotte out. "Is there a phone I can use?"

Her hostess was all accommodating. As usual. "Certainly, dear Jan. In the library." A wave of Charlotte's hand gave the general direction.

Jan found it. She closed the door to give herself the illusion of privacy. The call couldn't wait until she got home. She needed to oil a few squeaky Ingraham family wheels before she could get her own life back. Once she did that, maybe things with Doug would fall into place as well.

Her father's voice was drowsy when he answered. "Wake me? Absolutely not, princess. The

261

ball game went into extra innings, that's all. I was just resting my eyes."

His usual story.

"Listen, Dad, can you get hold of Aunt Bea and Walter? I need to talk to one or both of them. I'll be home in half an hour. Have them call me then, will you? Yes, it's important. You will? You're a dream."

"All the girls say that," her father murmured.

When he got in his car and pulled back into the circular drive, Doug recognized Jan's Oldsmobile tucked off to the side of the road. He hadn't seen her at the party. But if she'd seen him, she'd probably ducked out to avoid him.

Could he really blame her? She thought he was as much of an opportunist as Jason. Probably didn't even realize that Jase had always been one to begin with.

He couldn't tell her either. It would sound like sour grapes on his part. Like he was trying to take her in. Again. So he'd lost the girl of his dreams. He'd got a little satisfaction from punching Holloway. But he was still alone in his coaching house.

Perhaps time would ease the pain. Perhaps he'd meet another wholesome girl who claimed she wasn't domestic but who baked her own bread and made apple butter each fall. A girl who knew her way around a graphics table but preferred collecting dead vines.

Damn, how the hell was he supposed to forget her when he had a whole miniature forest full of the damn things on his property?

She was lost to him. He knew it as surely as he knew there would never be another woman like her in his life.

Doug turned his car east, turned his back on Richmond. He lived on the Ohio side of the line now. He'd damn well stay put there, far from temptation.

Three weeks went by before the temptation became too much to bear.

He had filled a custom order for a decorator who wanted one of his more whimsical dragon and maiden sculptures, and had replenished his coffers on the extravagant price he'd set. Fortunately, there were a good number of people willing to pay any amount for his creations. This time the maiden in the dragon's talons had resembled Jan Ingraham and he'd given the dragon a name. The client had been pleased and amused by the title of the sculpture—*Damsel in the Grip of L'Amour.*

After the piece was shipped, he finished sanding the last of the coach house's floors, revarnishing them, and polishing them till they shone like mirrors. He patched the plaster walls and repainted. The smell was enough to keep him high for days.

Perhaps that was why he decided to call.

Doug stared at the phone. Picked it up. Set it back down. Picked it up again.

His fingers shook slightly as he dialed the number. He didn't breathe at all while it rang. Four horrendously long peals. Then Jan's sweet voice came on the line.

"Hello."

"Jan, I . . ."

"I'm not available at the moment. Please leave your name and number at the tone," her recorded voice continued.

When the electronic beep sounded, Doug carefully replaced the receiver. The only message he could leave she wouldn't believe. Even though he really did love her.

When the phone rang, Jan let it go unanswered. There was a nice crosswind running through the kitchen from the open windows. She continued to sit at the table painting the faces on her elf ornaments. In the empty front room, the sound of the phone echoed.

She hadn't picked up a call in a long time. Usually it was just her mother checking on her, or a charity asking for a donation, or a sales pitch for carpet cleaning. The machine monitored everything. When she recognized her mother's voice, she picked the phone up. Otherwise, she let it ring. She didn't care if the caller was irritated by reaching a machine.

She heard her own voice run through the recorded message, thought she caught the sound of someone calling her by name. A voice she recognized.

It couldn't be. She wanted him to call so badly she was imagining things.

The brush was poised over an elf, the paint drying in the breeze. The beep sounded. She thought she heard a man clear his throat.

Great! An obscene call. Just what she needed now that her life was falling back into its familiar groove.

No heavy breathing followed. No abhorrent suggestions. Just a sigh. And the sound of the connection being broken.

Jan leaped for the phone, sure, now that it was too late, that she had just missed the long-awaited call.

"Doug?" she gasped into the receiver. The dial tone buzzed in her ear.

Damn and double damn! And . . . *damn!*

How the hell was she supposed to apologize if she had no idea how to reach him? Jason hadn't seen Doug since the night of Charlotte's party. There was no forwarding address at his old apartment. He hadn't stayed long enough to generate local mail. She'd tried writing a letter. It had come back, addressee unknown.

Jan stared at the phone willing him to call back.

The paint caked on her brush unnoticed.

* * *

265

Doug tried a second number. It was answered by a crisp voice nearly before it had completed the first ring.

"Penn Graphics," it said. "This is Judy. How can we help you?"

Doug stared at the receiver in surprise. "Ah, sorry," he mumbled. "Wrong number."

What had happened to L'Amour? When had she sold it? And why to Charlotte Penn?

He couldn't sit still, couldn't concentrate on anything. His work pedestal was set up, the clay ready. And he hadn't had even the glimmer of an idea of what to create. All he could think of was Jan.

So Doug did what he'd done nearly every day since moving onto the property. He walked into his private woods, leaned against a tall tree, stared at the wild growth around him, and thought about her even more.

Ten days went by before he worked up courage to call again. The closest he got to her was the recorded message.

The station wagon pulled up the long drive, the radio blaring, the preschoolers in the back squealing over who got to hold a pink teddy bear.

Jan looked over her shoulder at the two rosy-cheeked towheads. She'd just learned her first lesson in having children. Never buy two *different* things. Always buy two of the same.

"I warned you," her cousin Carrie said with a wide grin. She shoved the gearshift into park and unsnapped her seat belt, her long blonde hair swaying.

"I know you did," Jan muttered. "Maybe if *we* fought over the blue bear, one of them would take a liking to it."

Carrie chuckled. "Steve and I thought of that. It didn't work. *And* he wouldn't let me keep the purple unicorn even after I won the contest."

Jan got out of the car, slammed her door shut, and opened the one to the middle seat. She reached over Steve Jr., a sturdy three-year-old, and pulled the toy out of his hand. "Mine," she said.

Diverted temporarily, both children laughed at her. Their blue eyes sparkled with health and happiness.

Carrie unbuckled her two-year-old daughter, Lindy, from the car seat. She tucked the ignored powder blue toy under her arm. "I think I hear your phone ringing, Jannie. Go catch it. I'll take care of the kids."

Jan poked a finger in Stevie's round tummy. "The machine will catch it," she said and freed her little cousin from his restraints. The boy bounded into her arms, latching onto the pink toy at the same time.

"I envy you, Carrie," Jan said straightening up, the toddler squirming in her arms. "You've

267

got a great husband, beautiful children. Heck, even a station wagon. And now you're going back to work as a CPA, too!"

Carrie laughed. The sound was as carefree as that of her little ones. "Yep, everything I wanted."

Since Stevie was still squirming, Jan set him down. He immediately set off for the swing on the front porch.

"Now you'll get even more than you wanted. We still take the same size, don't we?" Jan asked. "I've got a closet full of suits from my unsuccessful management days. I'll never have a use for them now. You've welcome to all of them."

"You're sure?"

At Jan's fervent nod, Carrie accepted the full dozen.

"What about you, Jan?" Carrie asked. "When we were girls you always wanted to be a great artist. What happened to your dream?"

The two women walked side by side back to the house. Rather than fix lunch, they'd taken the children to McDonald's for Happy Meals, then stopped at a local card shop. That had been the mistake of the day. The pink and blue bears had sat side by side at the register. When Jan had spotted them, she'd immediately bought them for the children.

Which only showed how ignorant she was, Jan figured.

"My dream? It got altered by reality, Carrie."

It was Lindy's turn to squirm now, insisting

268

her mother let her down so she could get on the porch swing with her brother.

"And this is it? The new dream?" Carrie asked with a gesture that took in the farmhouse and the hastily moved crafts. The ornaments had especially taken the children's fancy. Upon their arrival the tikes had asked sweetly if they could each have one of the people cookies. And a glass of milk.

"The dream? Sorta," Jan admitted. "Not too dazzling, is it."

"As long as you're happy," Carrie said, although she didn't sound very convinced. "I think you need a family of your own."

Jan chuckled. "You and Mom and Dad. Even Aunt Bea has mentioned it now that she's a married woman."

Carrie wrinkled her nose. "Ha. Bea and Walter have been carrying on for years. She just wasn't sure if it was her or Uncle Simon's business that kept Walter turning up on the doorstep."

They both sat down on the top step, half turned toward each other.

"Of course, it wasn't Simon or Bea or Walter who made everyone happy," Carrie said. "It was you."

Just as she had each time a member of the Ingraham clan had tried to thank her, Jan shrugged it off. "It's not like I gave it all away," she insisted. "I did keep the lion's share."

Carrie snorted. "A piddling amount."

"An eighth. Same as Dad and Bea got. The

rest was divided up between fifteen of you."

"It was still a godsend as far as Steve and I are concerned," Carrie said. "We had the down payment for the house of our dreams, and have some put aside for the kids for college." Then she turned quickly to where her offspring were about to do damage to each other again. "Stevie, you're pushing that swing too fast."

Jan got to her feet. "How about some iced tea? I've had a jar of sun tea brewing since early morning. Fixed it special when you called from Indy."

"I thought you needed a warning before I visited with my brats," Carrie said. "I'd love some."

"Be right back," Jan declared and went into the house.

If she wasn't going to answer the phone, Doug swore, slamming the receiver down, well, she could just go to hell for all he cared.

He stared out the window at the woods.

No, she couldn't. He was too miserable without her to consign Jan Ingraham anywhere but where she belonged. At his side.

Okay. A physical showdown then.

Doug grabbed his keys, slammed the door, and headed west on the National Road. Half an hour later he turned onto the street that led to Jan's farmhouse.

What should he say to her? Would she slam the door in his face? Would she even answer his knock?

He cruised slowly, inching down the road hoping a plan would come to mind. He was almost at the gravel drive when he realized that things were even more wrong than he'd thought. Jan's Oldsmobile wasn't parked alongside the farmhouse. A white Plymouth Voyager and a metallic blue-green Chevy station wagon set in the drive. On the porch a blond woman pushed two blond children in the porch swing.

My God! Jan didn't even live there anymore!

Doug pulled on down the street, wove his way back through the housing development to the highway and crossed the Ohio line again. He did it all without conscious thought. There was only one refrain playing through his head.

How was he ever going to find her again?

August ended but the weather stayed warm into the first weeks of September. Doug pushed the windows wide at his coach house. It wouldn't be long before the trees in the woods at the back of the property began to display their multicolored fall coats.

He had a number of new commissions for statuettes. Clients were planning special holiday gifts. He'd managed a couple of uncommissioned pieces as well, one an ethereal wood nymph bedecked in artistically entwined grapevines. He'd never sell that one, he promised himself.

Now that the repairs on the house were completed, he was anxious to open his gallery. But he didn't have enough of his own work to fill it. Even if his ego had demanded a solo showing.

The hated siding on the outside of the house was gone. Prying it off had been back-breaking, but it had been great therapy for keeping his mind from brooding about a future without Jan. Beneath the siding he'd found beautifully weathered red brick. Now, lovingly cleaned and touched up, it restored the house to its original beauty. The finishing touches outside had been the window and door sills. Scraped, sanded, resealed, and painted, they glowed a deep Federalist blue. For contrast, he'd slapped barn-red paint on the twin front doors. It had been the nearest match he could come to the natural beauty of the brick.

The house complete, Doug turned his attention to the parking area, leveling it, covering it with gravel, then bordering it with railroad ties.

After weeks of working alone at the grueling tasks, grilling his skin beneath the summer sun, Doug's muscles no longer complained about the toil. Occasionally he still gazed at the barn, half planning the renovations to be done. Or those he would have done if things had worked out differently. But since Jan had disappeared, the urgency to convert it had disappeared as well. The rooms above the gallery were enough for him. If the barn fell into an artistic ruin, well, so be it.

His life had to go on, even if at times he forced it.

The gallery would be his soul now. But it was

lifeless until he found the artists and artisans to fill it. With that in mind, Doug began getting the Sunday papers from Dayton, Columbus, and Akron. Sometimes, to get away from the crushing quiet of the secluded property, he spent hours driving to each of the three cities just to buy a newspaper. Each week he scanned them, looking for articles on local artists, for announcements of craft or art shows.

When the advertisements appeared for the Starving Artists Show in Miamisburg, the village south of Dayton, it sounded like the chance of a lifetime. Just the name of the show alone was encouraging. "Starving" artists were exactly the type of people he wanted in his gallery.

Doug waited until Sunday, the closing day, to go to the show. Many of the painters, sculptors, and crafts people would be looking at their left-over stock and disliking the idea of packing it back up. With a little luck, and some fast talking, he might be able to convince them to place articles—of his choice—on consignment at his gallery.

With decorator items available, he could officially hang his sign—Treasure on the Cumberland—and open for business.

The afternoon was bright and sunny, more like midsummer than early fall. Miamisburg was a charming little village that dated back to Ohio's pastoral past. The fair was held near the center in a timeworn park surrounded by homes that had patiently watched generation after generation pass through their portals. The trees were tall, broad, and still generously leafed. Paved paths wound from the edges of the park inward to the center. Doug parked on a narrow, crowded side street and strolled back to the show.

Booths crowded each other along the paths, offering visitors a wide selection of merchandise. Because the organizers of the fair insisted that exhibitors keep their prices below twenty-five dollars, most of the paintings were small. That didn't mean that the artists didn't have larger offerings at home in their studios. As Doug moved among the crowd, he left business cards, briefly explained the concept of his gallery, and asked if he could talk to the painters in the next week or so about their work. Within an hour, he'd lined up four painters and one potter as possible clients.

He was just cruising the last of the show when he spotted her. Her back was to him, but Doug had no trouble recognizing Jan's dark curls.

When a couple of laden shoppers bumped into him, Doug moved off the path into the grass. He stood stock-still afraid that his subconscious had conjured her up, that if he looked away, Jan would be gone.

Instead he heard the peal of her laughter. Doug offered up a silent prayer of thanks and edged closer.

Her booth was very simply arranged. A lattice-work screen created a back wall to which she had wired different styles of wreaths. A round table covered in a white ruffled cloth sat off to the side displaying sample dough ornaments, spoon dolls, and packages of potpourri. Around it large baskets nearly overflowed with other selections of the same merchandise. A folding lawn chair was edged into a corner of shade, a large thermos next to it in the grass.

In her worn jeans, high-topped sneakers, and feminine ruffled poet's shirt, Jan looked as fresh and delectable as a cool drink. More importantly, she looked like the girl he loved.

A couple of customers had stopped at her booth. One woman was debating the relative merits of two different wreaths. One was a twist of grapevines decorated with soft white and delicate pink wildflowers. The feminine shades were offset by some curling tasseled weed that he couldn't identify, and something that looked like dried teasel. Where the wreaths at other booths were decked with ribbons as well, Jan's boasted long spills of bleached dried grass. More wildflowers peeked from the trailing grass, continuing the color scheme. The other wreath combined milkweed pods, cattails, and thistles against what appeared to be loosely bound straw. The second customer was trying to choose a selection of dough ornaments and keep her six-year-old daughter from opening the packages of potpourri.

Doug sidled up behind the customers, making no effort to attract Jan's attention.

* * *

Jan bent down to the little girl's level to identify each of the ingredients in the potpourri,
keeping the child entertained while the women
made their decisions. Unlike some of her competition, pushing sales, even in the closing hours of
the show, had never appealed to her. She preferred to let her creations sell themselves. Which
they usually did. Her things were different
enough from the offerings at the other booths to
lure customers who had already purchased simi-
lar items from other exhibitors.

"You see this petal?" she asked the child,
pointing at one corner of the package.

"The pink one?" The little girl was very intent.
"What is it?"

"Part of a rose," Jan said.

The child pointed at another spot. "And the
white one?"

"A rose," Jan explained. "And so is the yellow
one and the peach one."

The little girl smiled softly and stabbed her
finger at the package. "And so is the red one?"

"Yep," Jan said. "When you put them all together they smell like a flower garden."

"Really?"

The child's mother made a motion. "Don't
pester the lady, Mitzi. I'll take these six," she
added, handing Jan a half dozen Santa's elves.
"Can you wrap them in something so they don't
scratch against each other?"

Slightly irritated that the woman would think

she was so careless with her own crafts that she wouldn't cushion them, Jan stayed at the child's side a moment longer. She might comb the woods for materials, but when it came to packing things, it looked like she had bought stock in a tissue paper factory.

"Of course, I . . ." Jan glanced up and saw Doug. She had to clear her voice, tear her gaze away, force herself to concentrate on the customer.

"Six," Jan repeated. "At five dollars apiece, that is . . ."

"Mommy, I want the rose stuff," the little girl whined.

"You'll just get it all over your room," the woman said, barely glancing at her daughter.

Jan stole a look at Doug. He wasn't smiling. He wasn't frowning either. And most of all, he wasn't turning away from her.

"I want it," the child shrilled.

The woman frowned and shook the girl's shoulder. "I said no."

"Mommy . . ."

Jan lost the rest of the high-pitched wheedling. "Excuse me," the second customer said, turning to tap Jan on the shoulder. "I'll take this one. That's twenty-five dollars. Do you take checks? I'm in a bit of a hurry."

"I won't spill it. I promise!"

"No, Mitzy. I believe I was first, miss."

"Whom do I make the check out to?"

"Mommmyyyy!"

"Do you want a spanking, young lady? Miss! I asked if you'd wrap those elves!"

Jan looked from the now crying child, to her mother, to the woman with the checkbook.

Her eyes met Doug's in a heart-felt plea.

A slow smile curved his lips, lit his eyes. "Sorry, I'm late, sugar," he said moving around behind the table and heading off the wreath customer. He reached for the grapevine, finding the bit of wire that held it on display. "Make it out to Janelle Ingraham. That's I-N-G-R-A-H-A-M."

Warmth seemed to rush through Jan's body. Her blood hummed. In the space of a heartbeat, her world had righted. With a quick grin at the sobbing child, she began wrapping each of the dough ornaments in bright red tissue paper. "How about if I throw the rose stuff in as a free gift?" she suggested and turned a brighter smile on the little girl's mother. "If you don't object," Jan added. "It's the end of the show, and you'll be doing me a favor. I wouldn't have to repack it."

The child's eyes were glistening with unshed tears. Her lips quivered.

Jan went on folding paper around each elf.

The woman sighed. "That's very kind of you. But I insist upon paying for it."

"Half price then," Jan offered and quickly totaled the purchases up.

More last-minute shoppers arrived, as if they had heard a clearance sale was in progress.

"Hi," Doug said softly from the corner of his

mouth as a couple of teenage girls oohed over the bags of potpourri.

"I could kiss you," Jan whispered, stepping around him to answer a question about one of the straw wreaths.

"I'll hold you to that," he answered, and accepted money from yet another customer for a couple of dolls and four bags of dried petals.

The sun was dipping behind the rooftops before the last of the shoppers disappeared from the paths. Jan's baskets were nearly empty. Only two wreaths still hung on the backboard.

Jan collapsed back in the folding patio chair, and blew an errant curl off her face. "Whew! I'm glad that's over."

"Good show?" Doug asked, his voice deceptively casual.

"Nearly four thousand total for the two days, I think."

This from the woman who had inherited over a million dollars. Thank God she hadn't changed from the girl he'd first kissed while posing for a book cover.

Doug whistled in admiration.

"My best yet," Jan admitted happily. "We're a good team."

As if he'd just heard his cue, Doug leaned forward, bracing the palms of his hands on the aluminum arms of the chair. "I always thought so."

Jan leaned forward, tilted her face up to his. "I've missed you."

"Really?" There was a smile in his voice. And

something very different, but decidedly nice, in his gray eyes. "I've been miserable as hell without you."

"Ditto," Jan confessed.

Doug's smile widened. "Now about that kiss . . ."

Jan slipped her arms around his waist and stood up. Doug's hands moved to her shoulders. "I've been thinking about that," she said. "And a lot more."

Epilogue

Doug cruised down Route 40 pleased with his life once more. Jan sat at his side, her eyes squeezed shut as he'd requested, a tender amused smile on her lips.

"I feel stupid," she said.

"Just a little farther," he answered. "I want you to get the full effect."

"Does the house have those two doors?"

"Wait and see."

He was still wearing the same clothes he'd put on the day before. After the Starving Artists Show he had been pleasantly surprised to find Jan was the owner of the Voyager. He'd helped reload it with her remaining merchandise, backboard, table, and baskets. She'd invited him back to her farmhouse for dinner. And breakfast.

Yes, life was just about replete.

He looked across the fields to his patch of untouched woods. Within moments he'd know if this feeling of contentment would be his for a lifetime.

"How much farther?" Jan asked.

"Almost there." He turned his car into the parking lot.

"Now?"

Doug pulled his door open. "Impatient, aren't you, sugar."

"Eager," Jan corrected.

"Keep your eyes closed. I'll guide you."

Jan sat quietly, a soft smile on her lips. She listened to his footsteps crunch the gravel. Somewhere nearby birds were trilling. There was the scent of fresh-mown hay in the air. But more important, there was a light fluttery feeling in her stomach. A feeling of anticipation. A slight touch of fear. She was poised on the brink of something of which she had no experience.

Doug opened the passenger side door, took her hand. "No peeping."

"Is it one of the places we visited together?" she asked.

"Nope. I found it the week after that. Easy. Step up." He guided her, his hands on her shoulders.

Jan felt the brush of tall weeds against her jeans, smelled the moist scent of growing things. The chirping of the birds was joined by the sound of insects humming, of squirrels chattering. She sensed the change in atmosphere as she moved from shade into sunlight and back.

"Almost there," Doug said.

"It's really back off the road, isn't it," Jan mused.

"This part is," he admitted. "Okay, you can open your eyes now."

She was almost afraid to.

At first the sunlight dazzled her as it dappled through the branches. It skittered down over the still-green leaves of a thicket of honey locust trees. A giant oak towered overhead, its limbs entwined with ropelike lengths of . . .

"Grapevines!" Jan breathed in surprise.

"Yep," Doug said. "And they can be all yours. For a price."

She turned to him, her eyes as wide and blue as the patch of sky just visible through the branches. "What kind of price?"

Doug settled his hands at her wrist. "A very dear one," he said. "You have to marry me to get your hands on those vines."

"Marry you," she repeated. Her arms slid around his neck.

"Soon," Doug added. "Very soon."

Jan's eyes strayed to the grapevines. They hung in splendid glory from the oak, twisted out to engulf the locust trees. They were sturdy enough for Tarzan to swing on.

"That's the only way I get them?" she asked, her voice reflecting a distinct longing.

Doug took her chin between his thumb and forefinger, turning Jan back to face him. "I'll throw in the honor of being one of the exhibitors in my art gallery," he said. "I've already done a three-dimensional portrait of you surrounded by them. And believe me, sugar, I

283

did justice to such a lovely subject."

Jan smiled at the teasing tone of his voice. "I suppose with all these enticements, I can hardly refuse. Of course, I realize you have an ulterior motive."

He tilted her face up, tipped his head. "Many, in fact."

"It's the home-baked bread, isn't it," Jan purred, her lips parted and close to his. She rose on tiptoe to be still closer to him.

Doug's arms tightened around her. "Not entirely."

"Ah." She sighed. "The apple butter I promised to make."

"Damn right," Doug said and kissed her.

CATCH A RISING STAR!

ROBIN ST. THOMAS

FORTUNE'S SISTERS   (2616, $3.95)

It was Pia's destiny to be a Hollywood star. She had complete self-confidence, breathtaking beauty, and the help of her domineering mother. But her younger sister Jeanne began to steal the spotlight meant for Pia, diverting attention away from the ruthlessly ambitious star. When her mother Mathilde started to return the advances of dashing director Wes Guest, Pia's jealousy surfaced. Her passion for Guest and desire to be the brightest star in Hollywood pitted Pia against her own family—sister against sister, mother against daughter. Pia was determined to be the only survivor in the arenas of love and fame. But neither Mathilde nor Jeanne would surrender without a fight. . . .

LOVER'S MASQUERADE   (2886, $4.50)

New Orleans. A city of secrets, shrouded in mystery and magic. A city where dreams become obsessions and memories once again become reality. A city where even one trip, like a stop on Claudia Gage's book promotion tour, can lead to a perilous fall. For New Orleans is also the home of Armand Dantine, who knows the secrets that Claudia would conceal and the past she cannot remember. And he will stop at nothing to make her love him, and will not let her go again . . .

SENSATION   (3228, $4.95)

They'd dreamed of stardom, and their dreams came true. Now they had fame and the power that comes with it. In Hollywood, in New York, and around the world, the names of Aurora Styles, Rachel Allenby, and Pia Decameron commanded immediate attention—and lust and envy as well. They were stars, idols on pedestals. And there was always someone waiting in the wings to bring them crashing down . . .

Available wherever paperbacks are sold, or order direct from the Publisher. Send cover price plus 50¢ per copy for mailing and handling to Zebra Books, Dept. 3978, 475 Park Avenue South, New York, N.Y. 10016. Residents of New York and Tennessee must include sales tax. DO NOT SEND CASH. For a free Zebra/ Pinnacle catalog please write to the above address.

OFFICIAL ENTRY FORM
Please enter me in the

Lucky in Love

SWEEPSTAKES

Grand Prize choice: _____
Name: _____
Address: _____
City: _____ **State** _____ **Zip** _____

Store name: _____
Address: _____
City: _____ **State** _____ **Zip** _____

MAIL TO: LUCKY IN LOVE
P.O. Box 1022C
Grand Rapids, MN 55730-1022C

Sweepstakes ends: 4/30/93

OFFICIAL RULES
"LUCKY IN LOVE" SWEEPSTAKES

1. To enter complete the official entry form. No purchase necessary. You may enter by hand printing on a 3" x 5" piece of paper, your name, address and the words "Lucky In Love." Mail to: "Lucky In Love" Sweepstakes, P.O. Box 1022C, Grand Rapids, MN 55730-1022-C.

2. Enter as often as you like, but each entry must be mailed separately. Mechanically reproduced entries not accepted. Entries must be received by April 30, 1993.

3. Winners selected in a random drawing on or about May 14, 1993 from among all eligible entries received by Marden-Kane, Inc. an independent judging organization whose decisions are final and binding. Winner may be required to sign an affidavit of eligibility and release which must be returned within 14 days or alternate winner(s) will be selected. Winners permit the use of their name/photograph for publicity/advertising purposes without further compensation. No transfer of prizes permitted. Taxes are the sole responsibility of the prize winners. Only one prize per family or household.

4. Winners agree that the sponsor, its affiliate and their agencies and employees shall not be liable for injury, loss or damage of any kind resulting from participation in this promotion or from the acceptance or use of the prizes awarded.

5. Sweepstakes open to residents of the U.S. and Canada, except employees of Zebra Books, their affiliates, advertising and promotion agencies and Marden-Kane, Inc. Void in the Province of Quebec and wherever else void, taxed, prohibited or restricted by law. All Federal, State and Local laws and regulations apply. Canadian winners will be required to answer an arithmetical skill testing question administered by mail. Odds of winning depend upon the total number of eligible entries received. All prizes will be awarded. Not responsible for lost, misdirected mail or printing errors.

6. For the name of the Grand Prize Winner, send a self-addressed stamped envelope to: "Lucky In Love" Winners, P.O. Box 706-C, Sayreville, NJ 08871.